THUNDER IN THE DAWN

By
HENRY KUTTNER

I0616708

ARMCHAIR FICTION
PO Box 4369, Medford, Oregon 97504

For more information about Armchair Books and products, visit our website at…

www.armchairfiction.com

Or email us at…

armchairfiction@yahoo.com

SUPERNATURAL FANTASY AT ITS VERY BEST!

Henry Kuttner's "Thunder in the Dawn" is one of the most exciting pieces of fantasy you'll ever read. It is set in ancient Atlantis and deals with Elak, the warrior prince who slew his father, the King of Cyrena, in a duel to the death. His younger brother, Orander, then inherited the thrown and Elak had gone into self-exile. But all was not well in Cyrena. A Viking invasion had upended the kingdom and Orander had been captured. But the Vikings did not stand alone. Behind their power was the magic of Elf, the most dreaded warlock in the whole of Atlantis. Elf's magic power held Orander a prisoner deep within the bowels of a crumbling, forbidden castle. And soon Elf sent a magically empowered assassin to slay Elak. Only the magic of a mysterious Druid priest stood between Elak and death. Together they set out to rescue Orander; but the way to Cyrena was choked with danger, both human and inhuman. And soon Elak and his companions were faced with one supernatural terror after another...

FOR A COMPLETE SECOND NOVEL, TURN TO PAGE 81

CAST OF CHARACTERS

ELAK

This exiled warrior had once been a prince. But he was still loyal to the kingdom—even if he had slain his father, the king.

LYCON

He wasn't much to look at, and he had too much love for the bottle, but he was fiercely loyal and willing to fight to the death.

DALAN

A gross-looking, brown-robed Druid priest. His magic was the only thing that stood between Atlantis and disaster.

VELIA

She was very beautiful and very much in love with Elak. She also was very married to one of the fiercest nobles in Atlantis!

ELF

He looked like an innocent young lad, but there was no doubt of the evil in this warlock's heart or the power of his magic.

GRANICOR

One of the more powerful nobles in Atlantis. Nothing stood between him and his possessions—one of which was his wife.

GUTHRUM

The leader of a band of Viking cutthroats who had overrun northern Atlantis. He had no fear of spilling enemy blood.

CHAPTER ONE
Magic of the Druid

The tavern was ill-lighted and cloudy with smoke. Raucous oaths and no less rough laughter made the place a bedlam. From the open door a cold wind blew strongly, salt-scented from the sea that lapped restlessly against the wharves of Poseidonia. A small, fat man sitting alone in a booth was muttering to himself as he drank deeply of the wine the innkeeper had placed before him, and Lycon's quick, furtive glances searched the room, missing no detail.

For Lycon was a little frightened, and this prevented him from getting drunk as quickly as usual. His tall friend and fellow adventurer, Elak, was hours overdue from a clandestine visit to a lady of noble blood, the wife of a duke of Atlantis. This alone might not have troubled Lycon, but he was remembering certain curious events of the past fortnight—an inexplicable feeling of being trailed, and an encounter with masked soldiers in the forest beyond Poseidonia. Elak's dexterity with his rapier had saved them both, and, later, he had attributed the attack to the soldiers of Granicor, the Atlantean duke. Lycon was not so sure. Their opponents had not been the swarthy, sinewy seamen of Poseidonia—they had been yellow-haired, fair-skinned giants such as were native to the northern shores of Atlantis. And for many moons Atlantis had been looking northward with apprehensive eyes.

The island continent is, roughly, heart-shaped, split down the middle by a waterway that runs from a huge bay or inland sea at the north down to a lake nearly at the southern extremity, thirty miles from the seacoast city of Poseidonia.

For as long as men could remember the northern shores had been harried by red-bearded giants whose long black galleys had swept down from the frozen lands beyond the ocean. Dragon ships they were called, and those who manned them were Vikings—sea pirates, plunderers who left ruin and desolation wherever they beached their craft. Lately rumors had spread of a great influx of these Northmen—and in taverns and by campfires men met and boasted and sharpened their blades.

There were two men in the brawling clamor of the inn who had attracted Lycon's intent gaze—one a gross, ugly figure clad in a shapeless brown robe, the traditional garb of the Druid priests. Beneath an immense bald head was a hairless, toadlike face glistening with sweat. These Druids, it was said, wielded immense power secretly, and Lycon habitually distrusted priests of any order.

Besides the Druid, Lycon watched a bearded giant whose skin showed traces of being darkened artificially and whose hair was probably dyed, as it showed blue in the lamp's glow. Casually the small adventurer touched the hilt of his sword. Somewhat reassured by the feel of its smooth metal, he banged his cup on the table and yelled for more wine.

"What watery swill is this?" he asked the innkeeper, a wizened oldster in a liquor-stained tunic. "It's fit for babes and women. Bring me something a man can drink, or—or—"

On the verge of uttering a grandiloquent threat Lycon subsided, muttering softly. "Gods!" he observed to himself as the innkeeper moved away, "what's got into me? These past weeks have made me a coward. I'll be jumping at shadows soon. Where in the Nine Hells is Elak?"

He paused to throw a gold piece on the table and to lift a replenished cup to his lips. That was but the first of many cups, and presently Lycon's apprehension and worry had crystallized into belligerency. The bearded giant was watching him, he saw.

Lycon drained his cup, set it down with a crash—and sprang to his feet, overturning the table. Dark faces were turned to him; wary eyes gleamed in the lamplight.

For all his fatness Lycon was agile. He leaped over the table and headed for the giant, who had not moved, save to set down his liquor.

Lycon was, by this time, very drunk indeed. He paused to drag his sword from its scabbard, but unfortunately it stuck, marring the impressiveness of the gesture. Nevertheless Lycon persisted and pulled out the weapon at last. He flourished it beneath the other's nose.

"Am I a dog?" he demanded, glaring malevolently at the giant, who shrugged.

"You should know," he said gruffly. "Go away before I slice off your ears with that toy."

Lycon gasped inarticulately. Speech returned with a rush.

"Misbegotten spawn of a worm!" he snarled. "Unsheathe your sword! I'll have your heart out for this—"

The blackbeard cast a swift glance around. He did not look frightened, but, oddly, annoyed, as though Lycon had interrupted some important project of his own. Yet he stood erect, and his blade came out flashing. The inn-keeper hurried up, clucking his annoyance. In one of his hands was a bungstarter, and watching his chance, he brought this down toward Lycon's head.

From the corner of his eye the little man saw the movement. He ducked, whirled, felt his shoulder go numb beneath the blow. The giant's sword swept out at his unprotected throat.

Something hit Lycon, sent him sprawling back, while razor-sharp steel raked his chest. He fought frantically to regain his footing. He came upright with his back to the wall, sword in hand—and stood staring.

Elak had at last arrived. It was his blow that had hurled Lycon from the path of the giant's steel, and now the lean, wolf-faced adventurer's rapier was engaging the blackbeard's weapon in a dazzling flash and shimmer of clanging metal, while Elak's laughter brought fear to his opponent's eyes. The innkeeper crouched nearby, the bungstarter gripped in his hand, and swiftly Lycon caught up a heavy flagon and crashed it down on the man's head. He fell, blood spurting, and Lycon turned again to watch the battle.

The blackbeard was being forced back by the rapidity of Elak's onslaught. Few could stand successfully against the electric speed with which the adventurer wielded his rapier; already the giant was bleeding from a long cut along the forehead. He cried, "Wait! Wait, Elak—"

And his sword came down, leaving his throat unprotected.

But Elak also lowered his rapier. His wolfish face cracked in an ironic grin.

"Had enough?" he taunted. "By Ishtar, but you've little courage for your size."

The giant fumbled with the fastenings of his tunic.

Abruptly he brought out something thin and dark and writhing coiled about his arm. He flung it at Elak.

The rapier screamed through the air but missed its mark. Elak sprang aside just in time; the dark thing shot past him and arched up to avoid the swinging cut of Lycon's sword. For a brief moment it hung in empty air, while the silence of stupefaction stilled the tavern's clamor.

It was a serpent—but a winged serpent! A snake with two webbed, membranous wings sprouting from its body. Beady eyes glittered in the triangular head as the monster hung aloft. Then down it came, swift as an arrow's flight.

Chairs and tables crashed over, and the thunder of frantic feet sounded. Lycon's thrust almost spitted Elak. The winged snake, unhurt, flashed away, but its fangs had grazed Elak's shoulder. The brown leather of his tunic darkened swiftly, while a stench of foul corruption was strong in his nostrils.

"Bel!" he ground out. "I can't—"

Suddenly a bulky figure loomed before him—the Druid, huge arms lifted, shielding the adventurer with his own body. Elak made to thrust him aside. Then, staring, he paused.

From the upthrust hands of the Druid a pale flame was rising, twin fires that burned fiercely, dwarfing the yellow glow of the lamps. Incredibly the flames swelled and grew and abruptly took flight. The winged serpent twisted in midair, its wings shirring. But inexorably the flames raced down upon it.

They spread out lambent fingers, interlacing, till around the monster revolved a sphere of silently glowing fire. The serpent was hidden from view by a glove of flame.

And it swiftly diminished, shrank to a tiny glowing point— and vanished. Where flame and serpent had been was nothing. A gray dust filtered slowly to the rough planks of the floor...

CHAPTER TWO
Northmen in Cyrena

"So may all traitors die!" the Druid said harshly.

He was staring at an outsprawled giant figure that lay broken across a splintered table, a man whose black-bearded, swarthy face was upturned to the lamplight. On his brow a circle of reddened skin was burned and blistered, and blood bubbled in his throat.

Before either Lycon or Elak could move, the Druid had bent above the dying man, gripping his hair with rough fingers.

"Who sent you?" he snarled, his toadlike face aglisten with sweat. "Tell me, you dog—or I'll—"

"Mercy!" the wretch gasped, blood gushing from his mouth.

"I'll give you such mercy as will send your soul screaming down the Nine Hells! Who sent you? Tell these men!"

The man croaked, "Elf! He—"

Callously the Druid turned away. A frown creased Elak's brow as he saw the fear-glazed eyes roll up in death. "Elf?" he repeated. "I know that name."

"You should," the Druid growled. "Perhaps you know mine, then—Dalan. Come on, we've no time to talk. The guards will be here in a moment."

Lycon hesitated, shrank back. But Elak gripped his arm and urged him in the wake of the Druid.

"We can trust him," he whispered. "I've heard tales of this Dalan. And I think—" There was a wry smile on Elak's lean face. "I think we'll be safer with him than anywhere else."

A wan moon hung low over Atlantis. Keeping in the shadows, the three cautiously made their way along the waterfront. Once they shrank back into a doorway while a troop of guards clattered past. And at last they came to a low hut into which Dalan ushered them, barring the door carefully before he turned to take a lantern from a peg on the wall.

Even then he paused to lift a trapdoor in the floor before setting the lantern on the rough table in the center of the bare, gloomy room. "In case of surprise," he explained; "though I think we're safe enough here."

"In Bel's name, what's this all about?" Lycon demanded. The drink was wearing off, and he was trembling a little with reaction. Gratefully he sank down in a chair the Druid indicated. "Did you kill that bearded swine? Winged snakes—magic fires—haven't you anything to drink in this cavern?"

"You'll need a clear head for what I'm going to tell you," Dalan said. "There's magic in it, yes, or at least a science you can't understand. I slew that traitorous dog with a power we Druids have had for ages—a power over fire. And thus I slew Elf's messenger."

"The snake? Who is this—Elf?" asked Lycon.

Dalan sent a somber glance toward Elak, whose face was grim and cold. He asked, "This man—does he know nothing? Have you told him of Cyrena?"

Elak shook his head. "Tell him, Dalan."

"Cyrena? The northermost kingdom of Atlantis?" Lycon asked. "I know Orander rules it, but that's all."

"A dozen years ago Norian ruled Cyrena," the Druid said. "He had two stepsons, Orander and Zeulas. Zeulas killed Norian."

Elak moved uneasily.

"Zeulas killed him," Dalan repeated, "in fair fight and both men had provocation. Because of this, Zeulas, though he was the elder, did not assume the crown. He left Cyrena to wander, a homeless vagabond, through Atlantis."

Lycon turned to stare at Elak. "By Ishtar! You don't mean—"

"He is Zeulas," the Druid said, nodding toward Elak. "His brother, Orander, rules over Cyrena. Or—did rule."

"The Vikings?" Elak asked.

"Yes. They've invaded the land, with the aid of Elf the warlock. Elf has always hated your brother, who would never give him the freedom he wanted for his black sorcery and human sacrifice. So Elf made a pact with the Northmen to destroy Orander, in exchange for power and for the victims he needs for his necromancy."

"Did he—" Elak did not finish, but a cold fire blazed in his eyes.

"He couldn't kill Orander; my magic was too strong for that. But he has taken him captive and left the armies of Cyrena without a head. So the chiefs argue and battle among themselves, and the Vikings slay them at leisure."

Lycon was nearly sober now. A smoking oath came from his throat. "Your kingdom, Elak? This is your kingdom? And the Northmen and this stinking wizard rule it? Dalan..." He stood erect, teetering a little. "...we head north tomorrow—tonight! I'll slit this Elf's throat like a pig's."

Elak pulled him down. "Wait a moment. Dalan—you want me to return to Cyrena? To lead the armies against the Vikings?"

The Druid nodded. "That's why I'm here. Elf caught me unawares, and he has your brother captive. But if you'll come north, you'll give Cyrena the leader it needs. My magic will aid you."

"To free Orander?"

"Yes. And to destroy Elf, to drive out the Northmen!" The toad face grew hideous with rage. "They desecrate the Druid altars, crucify our priests! They worship Loki and Thor and Odin, devils of the blackest abyss—and they worship Elf's evil gods, as well. By Mider!" Dalan's hand moved in a strange quick gesture as he named the Druids' greatest deity. "You'll come—you must come, Zeulas— Elak—whatever you name yourself now!"

Elak stood up. "Yes, I'll come. I'd sworn never to enter Cyrena again, but this is a different thing."

"And I'll go with you," Lycon put in. "You'll need a strong sword in the forests. It's a far distance to Cyrena."

"Good!" Dalan's great hands swept down, gripped Lycon's shoulders. "You have courage—and you'll need it. But we'll not go through the forests. Look…"

He bent to scrawl, with a bit of charcoal, a rough map on the table's top. "Here we are at Poseidonia. We go inland thirty miles to the Central Lake, where I've a ship waiting. Then north, down the river through the heart of Atlantis, into the Inland Sea that touches Cyrena. We'll go with the current, and my oarsmen are strong."

"And we start—" Lycon's face was eager.

"Tomorrow, at dawn. You'll stay here with me tonight."

Elak hesitated. "Dalan, we may not return. And I promised—well, there's a girl I'll have to see tonight."

"Velia?" Lycon asked. "Duke Granicor's wife? I should think you'd had enough of her by now. And, by the way, what kept you tonight?"

"Her kisses," Elak said frankly. "I told her I'd see her before leaving Poseidonia."

Dalan grunted, "The guards—"

"I can evade them."

"What about the man I killed in the tavern tonight—and Elf's messenger? I tell you, Zeulas—or Elak—Elf fears you.

He knows I came to Poseidonia to bring you north to fight him, and he knows, too, that if you're dead, the Vikings will sweep unopposed over Cyrena. He has servants besides the Northmen—renegades, traitors!"

"I see Velia tonight," Elak said stubbornly. He turned toward the door.

"Wait." Dalan's huge hand spun him about. "There's no need to take unnecessary risk. We'll leave tonight—and, on the way, you can stop for a kiss or two with this wench. But you're a fool to do it."

"It isn't the first time women have made a fool of Elak," Lycon said, grinning. "But Dalan's right. We'd better leave Poseidonia now. I'll feel safer in the forest."

Elak shrugged and waited while the Druid hastily erased the map from the table. That done, the three cautiously let themselves out into the moonlit alley...

The palace of Duke Granicor shone whitely, towering on a hillock above Poseidonia. To the southeast the ocean swept out to a dim horizon. In the other direction was the forest, dark, menacing. In the shadow of a gate Lycon and Dalan waited while Elak dexterously mounted the wall. He moved quietly through the perfumed blossoms of the garden till he reached the trellis beneath Velia's window.

He had climbed it often before, and it gave no trouble now. The girl came upon the balcony as he softly called her name. He was briefly silent, studying her golden beauty in the moonlight.

Her transparent robe concealed little; she seemed like an amber statue draped in gauze. Bronze hair fell disheveled about an oval, elfin face; amber eyes were upturned questioningly to Elak's. Without a word he drew her close.

"I'm leaving Poseidonia," he said after a time. "I may not see you again for a while."

She clung to him. "Elak, I wish—I'll go with you!"

"No. You—"

"I will! I can't stand it here with Granicor. He's a beast, Elak—a devil. You know how he bought me from my father—I'm little better than a slave to him. I—I'd have killed myself if I hadn't met you."

"Don't be a fool," Elak said gruffly. "You'll get used to him in time. Though, by Ishtar, his face is enough to frighten babies! Well—"

"You're frank, at least, vagabond," a new voice growled. "And you'll be franker on the rack, with this harlot beside you!"

Elak released the girl and swung about quickly to face the man who came on to the balcony from the shadows. Duke Granicor was smiling, baring stained, discolored teeth through a gray-shot beard. In his silks and velvets he looked incongruously bedecked, a huge ape masquerading in borrowed finery. Bloodshot small eyes glared at Elak from little pits of gristle.

"You skulking dog!" Duke Granicor roared, lifting a dagger. "Your face'll frighten soldiers when I'm through with you!"

From the garden below came the clash of armor and the swift thud-thud of racing feet.

CHAPTER THREE
Through the Black Forest

Elak had no time to draw his rapier before Granicor was upon him. He twisted lithely beneath the dagger's blow, felt the blade tear and scrape along his ribs. Then he closed with his opponent, grimly silent.

Granicor's arm rose up, blade red and dripping, but before it could descend Velia had gripped it. Before the duke could wrench his weapon free the girl had bent swiftly, set her teeth in hairy flesh. Granicor roared an oath; but the dagger dropped, went clattering over the rail to the garden below.

Someone was climbing the trellis. Elak dropped swiftly beneath Granicor's encircling arms, and his own sinewy arms went about the duke's knees, gripping them tightly. With one swift movement he hurled himself up and back, sent his opponent crashing over the marble balustrade, hurtling down into the shadows. A yell of alarm and a scrambling in the foliage, ending in a smashing thud, told of a guard wrenched from his perch by Granicor's descending body.

Elak seized Velia's hand. "Come on," he snapped, and dragged her from the balcony within the room. A glance told him that there were no enemies here. Apparently the duke had been alone, save for his cohorts in the garden.

Now Velia took the lead. "I know the palace," she said swiftly. "There's a door Granicor may have overlooked. If there's no guard—"

They sped along dimly lit halls draped with tapestries and rugs of somber magnificence. Faintly there came to Elak's ears the sound of men's voices shouting. Into a narrow hall—down a steep winding staircase...

Elak gripped a heavy iron door, flung it open. Someone rose up before him, startled and menacing; armor glinted in the moonlight. But the slim rapier sheathed itself in flesh, and blood spurted from a pierced throat as the guard sank down groaning. They hurdled his body and raced into the garden.

Blades shimmered frostily; shadows closed in on them, Elak saw Granicor, his face blood-smeared and horrible, one arm dangling uselessly, bellowing commands to his men. But surprise was in their favor, and they made the gate safely.

To their surprise it was open. Elak pushed the girl through and turned to find the pack yelling at his heels.

Huge hands gripped him; he was drawn through the gateway. Metal clanged. The gross figure of the Druid stood briefly between him and the soldiers. Then, without warning, a tongue of fire licked up from the ground. It spread and lifted, filling the gateway with its red blaze. Dalan turned.

"That will stop them," he grunted, "for a time, anyway. Hurry!"

Lycon came out of the shadows, and the four raced into the dimness, seeking shelter in a nearby grove of trees before Granicor remembered to use arrows. As they came panting among the shielding trunks a menacing roar came from the palace, and a rout of men, armor glittering, came pouring down the hill.

"More than one gate," Elak muttered. "Well, shall we fight—or run?"

"Run," Lycon advised. "I'll stay here and hold them, for a while, at least. You can—"

The Druid whispered, "Come. I know the forests. Follow me—and they'll never find us. You too, Lycon."

Velia's hand was warm in Elak's as they silently trailed Dalan. Like a shadow for all his gross bulk the Druid slipped from tree to tree, taking advantage of every bush and shrub, till at last the noise of pursuit died in the distance. Only then did he pause to wipe the sweat from his ugly face.

"No enemy can find a Druid in the forests," he informed the others. "If necessary, our magic can send the trees marching against those who follow."

Elak grunted skeptically. "Well, I've let us in for something now. Velia's coming with us. I'm not going to leave her here to be skinned alive by Granicor."

She pressed closer to him, and Elak's arm went about her warm slimness.

"It's no hardship," Lycon said, glancing slyly at the girl. "And my sword is yours to command."

Velia thanked him with a glance, and the little man expanded visibly. Elak's expression was none too cordial.

"Let's get started," he said. "We've a long march to the Central Lake and your ship, Dalan."

The Druid nodded and took the lead. They set out through the moonlit forest...

Presently the moon sank, but Dalan guided them unerringly, even in the vague starlight, where they would have been separated had they not joined hands. Weird noises came out of the night; the shrill calling of birds and the rustle of underbrush. Once the ground shook beneath the tread of some giant beast that lumbered past unseen in the gloom. And once Elak spitted with his rapier a spider as large as his hand, which squirted venom a dozen feet as it writhed and died.

As dawn came they reached the Central Lake, a chill blue expanse whose depths had never been plumbed. Zones of sapphire and aquamarine and deeper blue lay across its surface. Floating at anchor not far away was a long galley, sails furled, waiting.

Sand crunched beneath their sandaled feet as the four hurried to the water's edge. Dalan made a speaking-tube of his hands and bellowed lustily till a small boat left the galley, heading shoreward.

"That's done, at least," Lycon said with satisfaction. "My poor feet!"

He sat down and rubbed them tenderly. His own sandals had gone to protect Velia's feet, but the girl's flimsy nightrobe had been ripped to shreds by thorns and branches. She kicked off the sandals, slipped out of her garment, and ran into the lake, laughing with pleasure as the cool water caressed her aching muscles.

Lycon eyed her enviously. "I'd join her if I had time," he observed. "Well, a few buckets of water will do the trick on deck. Here's the boat."

Two oarsmen rowed it; Dalan greeted them and quickly clambered aboard, his brown robe fluttering in the breeze. The others joined him; Lycon and Elak and Velia, who, after a few abortive attempts to adjust her robe, gave up the effort and made it into a brief kirtle.

"You may swim along the shore," the Druid warned her, "but not out where the waters are deeper. This lake goes down to hell itself, I think, and there are devils below its surface."

Lycon stared curiously around, apparently disappointed because no devils appeared. Then he fell to polishing his sword...

In the galley's pit men lounged on benches: brawny, half-naked oarsmen, not slaves, for they were not shackled to the benches. Dalan shouted an order as he climbed on board. Men scrambled to obey, settling in disciplined order, gripping their oars. A tall, broad-shouldered man with a golden collar mounted a platform. He gestured, cried a command.

The oars swept down, cleaving the blue waters of Central Lake. The galley sprang forward, plunging north.

North to Cyrena!

CHAPTER FOUR
Power of the Warlock

So the strong oars dipped and plunged, and the galley ran northward to where two shores converged in the river that cleft the heart of Atlantis, rushing between granite precipices, lazing through sunlit meadows thundering swiftly and more swiftly toward the Inland Sea and Cyrena. And these days seemed the happiest of all to Elak and Velia, while Lycon divided his time between drinking steadily and arguing with the overseer about navigation, a subject of which he knew nothing. Only over Dalan a shadow seemed to hang, and this grew darker as they swept north. When the sails were unfurled, they hung loose and useless, though storm clouds gathered each night to the south. At last Dalan called Elak to the cabin.

"Elf works magic," he said grimly. "Duke Granicor has not given up the pursuit. He sails after us with Elf's wizardry helping him."

Elak whistled between his teeth. "That's not so good. How do you know?"

Dalan lifted a dark cloth from a pedestal; light glinted from a crystal sphere large as Elak's head. "Look," he said, "I've known this for days..."

At first Elak saw only the transparent depths of the crystal, and very slowly, very gradually, they clouded and became translucent. Light images began to flash before his eyes, a vague succession of darting colors...and these crystallized into a scene, a tiny picture within the sphere: a galley, sails set and straining, racing between shores which Elak remembered passing only a day before. He looked up quickly.

"Wind? But our sails—"

"Calm follows our galley, but Elf's magic speeds Granicor's. We're nearly in the Inland Sea now though and—wait!"

Something was happening within the crystal. The sharply defined image shook and wavered, like a reflection in water. It misted and faded and changed—and a face swam into view: the face of a youth, rounded as a child's. Blue eyes, clear with candor, met Elak's; soft flaxen hair fell about the man's shoulders. And, for all the innocence of that cool gaze, Elak subtly sensed an ageless, malefic evil that dwelt within the blue eyes, a black horror utterly incongruous with the beauty of the face.

"Mider!" the Druid snarled. "Elf—watches us! He—"

The red lips parted in a singularly sweet smile. Dalan thrust his face down close to the crystal.

"Elf!" he roared. "Hear me! Ho, you stinking spawn of devils—hear me! Not all your foul wizardry can keep me from Cyrena, or the man I bring with me. Tell Guthrum that! Let him pray to Odin and Thor—and I'll grind their faces in the dust as I'll grind yours." He cursed the warlock bitterly, foully, while Elak watched fascinated.

The smile did not leave Elf's face. The crystal dimmed, grew cloudy—and was transparent. The vision had gone before Dalan paused in his tirade.

Sweating, he mopped at his gross face. "Well, you've seen Elf now. For the first time, eh?"

Elak nodded.

"What do you think of him?"

"I—scarcely know. He has my brother captive?"

"He holds Orander. And Guthrum, the Viking king, does as Elf wishes. You must fight Guthrum, Elak, as you would Elf. And Granicor's galley comes swiftly."

"I don't see why you fear him," Elak said. "Your own powers—"

"Are limited. And Mider knows what magic aids Granicor. D'you see that storm?" He gestured toward a porthole. Black clouds were drifting up from the south. "All the winds of hell are there—yet our sails hang without a breeze to lift them. Look..."

He turned to the north. "See that land, far distant? It's Crenos Isle, a place best shunned. We go past Crenos to Cyrena—but I think Granicor will find us first."

Dalan was right. The long galley of the duke swiftly drove before the storm, and just off the southern extremity of Crenos Isle the two ships met.

"One thing's in our favor," Dalan grunted, issuing weapons to the oarsmen. "Slaves man their oars. But ours are men, and warriors—men from Cyrena who'll not ask for quarter. But we have no fighting crew, and Granicor has."

"It's my fault," Elak said morosely. "If I hadn't got the duke on our trail—"

"Forget it!" Lycon swaggered up, brandishing his sword and exuding a strong aroma of spirits. "We'll run that dog up by the heels at his own masthead. Besides, Velia's a girl worth fighting for, by Ishtar!"

Velia, looking like a slim youth in her soft tunic, laughed almost gayly. "Thanks, Lycon. At least I'll not have to go back to Granicor. There are many ways to die here—to die easily."

"None o' that," Elak told her. "Though I suppose you're right. You can't enjoy life with your skin off. And that's the duke's favorite torture."

The sky darkened. Wind buffeted them. The oarsmen bent to their oars, swords at their sides. Granicor's ship lowered sail, but double banks of oars propelled it swiftly forward.

"They mean to ram," Dalan muttered. "Well, two can play at that game. Ready, now—"

He roared an order into the gale. Oars were lifted; the ship came around, and timbers cracked and groaned and shuddered at the shock as the galleys scraped almost prow to prow.

"Up oars!" Dalan bellowed. "Cast off grappling irons!"

His intention had been to cripple Granicor's galley by smashing one bank of oars, but he was too late. A dozen hooks snaked out, were drawn taut. The ships were locked together—and a wave of shouting, blood-hungry men came pouring over the gunwales.

"Get in the cabin," Elak commanded Velia, but she did not heed; there was a slim blade in her hand, and she stood coolly at his side. Dalan and Lycon flanked the two. The oarsmen seized their weapons, met the invaders. Swords clashed blindingly.

"Stay here, Lycon," Elak said suddenly. "Guard Velia." He sprang down into the pit among the mob of yelling swordsmen. A few arrows fell, but the galleys swayed and pitched so that accurate marksmanship was impossible. Still stronger came the storm wind, darker grew the clouds.

" 'Ware, Elak!" Lycon's voice.

The tall adventurer ducked a sweep of steel that came out of nowhere, saw a grinning swarthy face rise up behind him. The rapier danced into a dazzling shimmer, and the man went down coughing blood. Then Elak caught sight of Granicor fighting his way toward him, gray beard blood-spattered, shouting furious oaths. He sprang to meet the duke.

The ships heeled, rocked sickeningly in the trough of the waves. From the corner of his eye Elak saw a flicker of red fire, realized that Dalan was battling, too. The Druid's magic turned the tide.

Cold steel men could battle, but not this searing flame that sprang out of empty air to leave blistered corpses in its wake. The struggle went back to the gunwales, back and back to Granicor's galley, carrying Elak and the duke with it. Dimly Elak heard Dalan's exultant shout, the shrill cry of Velia...

Without warning disaster struck. A blast of frigid resistless air, a maelstrom of wind that smashed down on the two craft and ripped them asunder, sent them plunging through waters gone insane. Elak saw Dalan's galley being swept away, heard Granicor roaring in triumph as he plunged forward. He tensed for a leap, realizing as he sprang that he would fall short.

Salt water drove into his nostrils, choking him. He went down like a plummet, clinging grimly to his sword. Somehow he held his breath, fighting up toward a dim, hazily translucent green light. And somehow he kept afloat in a madness of racing seas, hanging to the fragment of an oar that drifted within his reach...but at last darkness took him, and he went down into the shadows.

Shadows that whispered, mocking him. Dim shadows, with cool blue eyes of Elf, moving swiftly in errands of mystery...vague visions of strangeness and of magic...and the faces of Velia and Lycon and the Druid, anxious and afraid. They were searching for him, he knew, and he tried to call a reassuring message. But the dreams faded and were gone...

CHAPTER FIVE
The Dwellers on the Isle

Elak awoke very slowly, conscious of a dull pain in his chest. A sudden gray sky lowered above him as he opened aching eyes. Nearby waves crawled up whispering on a slate-dark beach. He tried to sit up and discovered that his arms were bound tightly.

He turned to see tall rocks hemming him in, monolithic eidolons that rose up in all directions save seaward. His attention was drawn by a flicker of movement to a slab of rock that towered twenty feet above him; there was a very narrow crevice splitting it, and from it came a man.

Elak could not repress a start. Before him was a Pikht—a member of the almost legendary race that had held Atlantis so many eons ago that their very existence had almost been forgotten. White men from the east had warred upon the Pikhts, exterminating them ruthlessly, until, on Crenos Isle, there dwelt what was probably the last survival of the race.

The man was dark-skinned and very short—scarcely five feet in height—and hairless. Not even his pale eyes were fringed by lashes. He wore no more than a loincloth, and great muscles crawled beneath the smooth skin. His somber face had an indefinably bestial cast, and Elak thought suddenly of tales he had heard of the kinship of Pikhts to the beasts—that these men were the first beings who had possessed the true human form, and who had possessed powers lost to those of a higher stage of evolution.

The Pikht bent over Elak, a knife in his hand. His voice was thick, guttural, and Elak could scarcely understand the Atlantean tongue he spoke. "Get up, stranger. Slowly!"

Elak, with some effort, got to his feet, careful to make no hasty movement. His rapier, he saw with regret, was gone. Also his legs were bound together by a thong about a foot long. The Pikht urged him toward the crevice in the rock. It narrowed until his broad shoulders scraped the side, then widened as he led down. Elak debated the advantage of trying to take his captor unaware, but, bound and unarmed as he was, he knew only death would result. Presently he felt stairs beneath his feet, invisible in the shrouding darkness.

" 'Ware!" It was the Pikht's harsh voice. "Not too fast!"

Obediently Elak slackened his pace. Before him a slit of light widened, and he looked down a corridor cut out of solid rock.

Perhaps two hundred feet long it was, lit by bronze lamps that stood in niches in the wall. Iron doors, with barred windows set in them, broke the monotony of gray rock on one side; the other side was blank, roughly chiseled stone. Elak paused.

The Pikht's blade gouged skin from his captive's back. Glancing around, Elak saw that behind the dark-skinned dwarf were two other men, replicas of his captor, hairless and smooth-skinned and dark. They carried long blades, longer than themselves.

Elak let himself be prodded along the passage. As he passed the barred doors he realized that they guarded captives, Atlanteans all, some clad in leather or armor, others in furry skins. In the silent faces that watched him Elak saw fear—fear so great that none spoke aloud. In whispers men cursed the Pikhts, and the dwarfs smiled mockingly, their eyes coldly alight with malicious amusement.

At a door near the end of the tunnel the Pikht halted. He gestured, and one of his companions lifted a great metal bar that locked the panel. The iron door was swung open, and Elak was thrust across the threshold.

Metal clanged; the bar was thrust into its socket. The cell, cut from solid rock, held nothing; but in the farther wall was another door—an iron slab whose smooth surface was featureless and unbroken.

Elak heard the Pikhts go padding along the passage. And, very slowly, the iron slab began to swing outward.

A man crept into the cell. His emaciated body was clad in a tattered jerkin, and tangled yellow hair hung about a bearded, pain-ravaged face. His eyes were vacuous filmed with a blue glaze. Spittle drooled from the slack mouth. Behind him the door swung silently shut as Elak sprang forward. He had only a flashing glimpse of a gray corridor—no more.

The man huddled in a corner, shuddering and moaning.

Elak looked down at him with pity. "Who are you?" he asked. "Can you understand me?"

"Yes…yes, I can understand. The Shadow took Halfgar, my son. The Shadow on the pool…"

The bearded face was contorted with grief and horror. Elak cast a swift glance at the iron door, cryptically shut. What talk was this of—a Shadow?

The blue stare focused on Elak. "Elf the warlock gave me to the Pikhts, and my son Halfgar went with me because he fought at my side against Elf's men. They—"

Elak leaned forward tensely. "Elf? These dwarfs—Pikhts—know him?"

"Yes; they serve him. They give him magic in return for strong men whom they sacrifice to their god. For ages they've dwelt on Crenos Isle worshiping—" The man's voice dropped to a thin reedy whisper, and madness crept into his eyes. "The Shadow took my son. The door opened, and I went out into the passage where the pool was. I saw water below me, and a Shadow lying upon it. The Shadow leaped up at me, and as I drew back it touched my brow...it was not hungry then. It had just fed on Halfgar...it took him from my side as I slept...there are doors which are not to be opened..."

The whisper stopped. The man's eyes widened. He sprang to his feet, clawing at his breast with ripping fingernails, tearing away skin and flesh in long ribbons. He screamed, a frightful, agonized shriek that resounded through the cell.

And he fell, a boneless huddle in the corner. His bearded face stared up blindly, and Elak saw that he was dead.

A soft rustling made him turn. Very slowly, very gently, the iron door was swinging outward. From the vagueness beyond the portal a misty gray light crept into the cell.

Elak heard the lapping of water...

Dalan's black galley lay beached on Crenos Isle, battered and bruised by the storm. The same gale that had flung the ship ashore had sent Duke Granicor's craft driving northward till it had been lost to view in the scud. Now the oarsmen were busy calking seams, mending the ruin the tempest had wrought.

But Dalan, in the cabin, crouched over his crystal globe, his ugly face set in harsh lines. Velia and Lycon stood beside him, curiously eyeing the sphere, watching the flashing images that swept through its depths.

"Elf's magic is strong," the Druid muttered. "He battles me at every step. But—"

"Is Elak alive?" Velia asked anxiously. "Why won't you tell me?"

"Because I don't know. Keep quiet, girl! Elf's spells war with mine, and I see nothing—yet."

He peered into the shimmering sphere. Lycon squeezed Velia's arm reassuringly. And suddenly Dalan expelled a long breath of relief.

"So! He lives—see?"

Within the crystal a picture grew, a tiny image of a beach flanked by towering gray rocks. On the slope a man lay bound and unconscious.

"Praise Ishtar!" Lycon said. "Is he far? I'll go after him—"

"Wait," the Druid commanded. "I know that beach. Elf's allies, the Pikhts, have an underground temple there. And—look!"

Velia gave a soft little cry. There was movement within the crystal; a man emerged from a cleft in one of the tall rocks and approached Elak's prostrate figure. As they watched they saw Elak prodded to his feet by the Pikht, urged into the darkness of the fissure. For a second the sphere was a ball of jet; then it brightened and showed a long corridor cut out of solid rock. Three dark-skinned dwarfs thrust Elak forward.

"Mider!" Dalan said tonelessly. "He's in the temple! And that means he's to be sacrificed to—"

"Not if I know it!" Lycon snapped. "How far is this temple? The crew have swords and know how to use them. Tell me how to go, Dalan—north or south?" He was at the door, grinning unpleasantly as he fingered the hilt of his blade. "I'll butcher those little devils for you!"

"Good! Go south, Lycon—and swiftly. You'll know the place.?"

"I'll know it. How far have we to go?"

"Half an hour's march, if you travel fast." The Druid turned to his globe. "I'll stay here. You must fight the Pikhts—but I battle Elf. And—" His huge hands swept down, gripped the crystal. "Hurry, Lycon! Elak's in danger now—deadly danger!"

Lycon thrust the door open, sprang on deck. His shrill voice shattered the morning calm. And in response the crew leaped to obey, dropping oar and hammer, taking up sword and ax, dropping over the rail to the beach. A half-naked, villainous-looking band, they trotted south, urged on by Lycon's searing oaths and the flat of his blade.

And with them came Velia, keeping always at Lycon's side, eyes flashing with battle-hunger, lips parted in a smile that was not pleasant to see. They went so swiftly that they reached their destination before the time Dalan had allotted. Recognizing the black cleft in the stone, Lycon halted his men to take the lead.

He stepped into the darkness with a strange crawling of uneasiness, sword bared, blinding in an attempt to pierce the gloom. Something moved, and he cut at a menace he sensed rather than heard. Steel gashed his thigh, but he felt his blade rip through flesh and grind against bone. A squealing, scarcely human cry sound. In a frenzy of loathing he struck and struck again, cutting his way forward against soft bodies that resisted briefly and then broke and retreated under his onslaught.

The oarsmen poured into the cleft, led by Velia, and in the darkness the Pikhts rallied and came at them, snarling rage. For a little while there was a black madness of battle, a chaos of yells and oaths and death cries. In the end Lycon won through, and the Pikhts scattered like rats before the sweep of thirsty blades.

Before Lycon now was a dim-lit corridor, one wall set with barred doors. He cut down a screaming dwarf that plunged at him, dagger bared, and left the rest to Velia and the crew. Swiftly he raced along the passage, casting hasty glances into each cell as he passed. Captives stretched out imploring hands, begging for release, but Elak was not among them.

Near the end of the corridor, one door was open. Lycon sprang over the threshold, saw a bare, empty cell with an iron slab ajar in the opposite wall. He went forward, sword dripping red on the stones as he lifted it.

Water was lapping softly nearby…

CHAPTER SIX
The Night of Gods

Elak stepped through the portal and found himself in a narrow passage. Gray light bathed him. In the distance he saw a sparkling surface that rippled in the cold glow.

And suddenly he heard Dalan's voice. It came softly from empty air, urgent, peremptory, calling his name.

"Elak! *Elak!*"

Searching the bare walls with incredulous eyes, Elak whispered, "Dalan? Where are you?"

The Druid's voice rang out sharply. "No time now, Elak—the Shadow comes as I speak. Leap into the pool—dive into it, now! At the end of the passage—" Still Elak hesitated. "But where are you—"

"There's no time to talk now! Hurry—"

The stark urgency of Dalan's words spurred Elak to action, sent him racing along the corridor. He checked himself sharply on the brink of a square basin. Little menace in that, or in the blue-green water that filled it. But within the pool dwelt horror. A Shadow lay upon it.

The shadow of a man, cast by—nothing! An opaque outline that lay incredibly on the surface of the pool. And it darkened into blackness, while the gray luminescence of the corridor dimmed.

" 'Ware, Elak!"

Dalan's voice, loud in warning! Elak whirled, saw a dark-skinned dwarf almost upon him, pale eyes blazing, bestial face menacing. In the Pikht's hand was a dagger.

The two men smashed together on the pool's brink, went down, clutching and tearing, the oily body of the dwarf squirming like a snake in Elak's grasp. Steel grated on the stones. Elak's fingers closed relentlessly on his opponent's knife wrist.

With a powerful lunge the Pikht brought his dagger down, its point touching Elak's chest. The two rolled over, snarling oaths, and—dropped into emptiness!

The pool took them—dragged them down into water icy as polar seas, blue as turquoise. Elak could see nothing but that illimitable blueness as he went down, choking for breath, battling against blinding panic. Was the pool bottomless?

The sapphire tint deepened to indigo, foamed in fantastic patterns before Elak's eyes. He realized abruptly that this was not water surrounding him—could not be, or he would have drowned minutes ago. There was a swift accelerating rush, and abruptly frightful cold, incredible agony, tore at the citadel of Elak's brain. He was conscious of a change.

Air rushed into his lungs—air stale and dead, as though it had never been breathed, yet curiously refreshing. Dim, flickering shadows were all about him. And the swarthy devil-mask of the Pikht's face swam into view from the vagueness.

Pale eyes glared into Elak's; the dagger came down viscously and buried itself in the ground as he writhed aside. He clutched at the dwarf's wrist, missed, and flung himself bodily upon the Pikht, bearing the smaller man down by his weight. But he could not maintain a hold upon the muscular, oily body.

Snarling, the dwarf lunged forward, teeth bared. Elak smashed his forehead into the Pikht's face, felt blood spurt into his eyes, blinding him. He shook the scarlet drops away.

Abruptly he released the Pikht's wrist. His hands shot up and gripped the dwarf's throat—sinewy hands that had been trained on battle-ax and rapier. The knife bit into his body, ripped flesh from his breast as he twisted desperately. But the Pikht had struck too late.

Elak's tapering brown fingers almost met in oily flesh.

Tendons stood out like rigid wires; there came a brittle cracking sound. A bubbling scream of agony died in the dwarf's throat before it could emerge.

The pale eyes glazed. The stunted body went limp.

Elak stood up, bracing himself. He stared in sheer astonishment.

It was no earthly landscape which he saw. Obscure color-patterns, shifting and dancing strangely, weaved in the cool air, all about him. He thought of the shadows of trees painted on white rock, flickering arabesques of dancing leaves fluttering in the wind. Yet the weird pattern was not only on the pale clay-colored plain on which he stood, but rather all about him in the air. He stood alone in a fantastic weave of somber shadows.

Colorless shadows, dancing. Or were they colorless? He did not know, nor was he ever to know, the color of the grotesque weavings that laced him in a web of magic, for while his mind told him that he saw colors, his eyes denied it.

Suddenly darkness swept down, engulfing him. And very faintly a thudding sounded, and swiftly grew louder. With a giant pounding of Cyclopean feet something strode past Elak in the blackness, something that shook the plain with the thunder of its passing. There was no other sound save for the tremendous booming thuds of the Titan feet.

They died in the distance; the darkness lifted. Again the flickering shadow patterns grew in the air. And again they darkened into blackness.

The sound of wings came to Elak. Something was flying far overhead, something that wailed endlessly and mournfully, keening the cry of one lost and wandering in eternal night. A sense of overpowering awe touched Elak, and horror beyond all imagination—the horror one feels in the presence of a thing so alien that the flesh of mankind instinctively shrinks and shudders. Elak knew, somehow, that he had entered a land in which men had not been intended to exist.

"*Elak...*"

Faintly, from very far away, the thin whisper came—Dalan's voice. Elak whispered the Druid's name as the darkness changed into the vague shadow-patterns. The distant voice came again.

"You are in a perilous place, Elak, but you live. Lycon's swordsmen slay the Pikhts now, the crystal tells me...you are very far away, Elak, but I come swiftly. Mider aids me..."

Blackness again, and a roaring as of great winds. Power unimaginable shuddered through Elak's body like a spear shattering on a shield. And it passed, and the darkness lightened to the crawling shadows.

"You are with the gods, Elak," came Dalan's far whisper. "You are no longer in Atlantis, or even on Earth. You are in a far land. And with you are those the Shadow has engulfed—the gods! Not the gods of Atlantis, nor the Viking gods, but the gods that have died. Around you move those whose flesh is not our flesh, whose lives are alien to ours. I come, Elak..."

Piercingly sweet, throbbing almost articulately, a harpstring murmured through the gloom. Dalan's voice faded into silence, and again the note sobbed out. Above it a soft-toned song lifted in the words Elak knew were in no earthly language.

Startled, apprehensive, the Druid called, "Elak! Elf's magic battles mine—he—"

Then silence, till a gentle voice spoke.

"Dalan," it whispered. "Dalan, Elak...my enemies. Now you shall die, Elak, for the Druid cannot reach you. The power of my harp keeps him from our side."

Very faintly Dalan called Elak's name. Once again he called and was silent. Shifting shadows moved through the dim air. Elak's hand went involuntarily to his side. Remembering that he was weaponless, he stooped and pried the dagger from the Pikht's cold fingers. But despair was mounting within him. How could he fight Elf, alone in this lost hell, without Dalan to aid him?

"Your doom comes," Elf murmured, and the harpstring twanged eerily, laden with bitter sweetness. "You live, Elak, and there is no life in Ragnarok. Only the dead gods, and the dust of the souls of men."

The dancing shadow-patterns slowed their fluttering and became motionless. The sound of Elf's harp died; it was utterly silent.

And, far in the distance and gigantic, towering above the horizon, a Shadow began to form in the air. In form it was human, but from its darkening nucleus there breathed chill horror that made Elak grip his dagger with desperate fingers. Fear shook him—the fear that attacks the citadel of man's soul when it faces the Unknown.

CHAPTER SEVEN
Solonala and Mider

A sound behind him made Elak turn swiftly, his weapon ready. What he saw made him pause in wonder. Even in the shadowy gloom he sensed something fantastically unreal about the figure that came stealing out of the dusk with curiously rocking gait.

But there was friendliness in the gesture with which the half-seen being beckoned. It glanced beyond Elak to where the Shadow grew and darkened on the horizon and then swiftly bent above the dead Pikht. Dark hands moved quickly—and suddenly the dwarf moved, raised himself stiffly to his feet, and stood motionless as an automaton!

The Pikht had died—that Elak knew. Even now the bald, misshapen head lolled monstrously on one sagging shoulder. Elak could scarcely see the dwarf's face, but he knew intuitively that the shallow eyes held no life. An icy shudder shook him.

The Pikht turned. Swaying, the squat figure raced forward, past Elak, toward the Shadow that loomed in black horror in the distance. A soft hand was thrust in Elak's, and he looked down to see a white girl-face peering anxiously up at him.

He felt himself being tugged along and yielded, smiling a little wryly. After all, into what worse hell could he be guided? The patterns flickered all around them as they moved, and presently Elak heard a low voice say, "We should be safe now."

"You speak Atlantean?" he asked involuntarily, and quiet laughter mocked him.

"I speak my own tongue. All languages are one here. Just as the Shadow appears differently to everyone and yet is the same to everyone after being—taken—so do all tongues seem alike here. The world from which I came is far from yours. How are you named?"

"Elak. The—Shadow?"

"It has faded. See?"

Elak glanced over his shoulder but could make out nothing but the dancing patterns of alien color. The invisible girl went on. "I put life into the dead being and sent him to the Shadow so that we could escape while the Shadow fed. We are safe for a little while, Elak."

She paused as the air lighted; they stood before a cave that opened into the side of a rampart which towered up until it was lost in the dimness. A misshapen, flat-topped boulder guarded the entrance of the tunnel mouth and behind this Elak's companion stepped swiftly.

"Come," she urged. "We can hide here—for a time at least."

But Elak had reached her side—had gripped her slim arms with fingers rendered cruel by his amazement. He stared at the girl in wonder, knowing that she sprang from no earthly race.

A satyr-girl! A faun-maiden, slender and white and virginal as cool marble, round-breasted, with red-golden hair that hung in velvet coils about the smooth shoulders. To her waist she was human. Below that all semblance of humanity ended, and sheer fantasy began.

Her legs were golden-furred and crooked like those of a beast—not ungainly goat legs, but rather the limbs of some graceful deer, ending in tiny hoofs that glinted golden in the dim light. Her face was as unearthly as her nether limbs, for all its classic beauty. No earth-girl had ever possessed *golden* eyes—eyes like flaky pools of pure gold, without white or pupil, that stared at Elak as unwinkingly as those of a cat. Her face was curiously feline in contour as she smiled at Elak, looking up at him fearlessly.

"I am strange to you?" she asked. "But you are strange, too. There are many worlds besides your own, Elak."

"So it seems," the Atlantean gasped. "By Bel! This must be some mad dream I'm having!"

The girl urged him further into the cave. A dim light irradiated its further recesses, which were draped with violet samite that hid the rough rock walls. Cushions carpeted and hid the ground.

"I am Solonala," the faun-girl told Elak, relaxing gracefully in a little nest of soft pillows. "Has Elf's magic sent you here, too?"

Elak did not answer; his eyes watched the eerie golden-furred legs in fascinated wonder. Solonala glanced down, smiling, and clicked her hoofs gently together. "We are made in different patterns, you and I."

Elak nodded. "Yes. Though—Elf, you say? D'you know him?"

"I know him, and I fought him. The land where I once ruled is far from here, and far from your own Earth. But Elf's powers enable him to go from world to world, and when he came to mine, I saw that he was evil and tried to destroy him. He was the stronger."

She shrugged slender shoulders. "So I came here, or rather Elf exiled me here. He couldn't kill me, for I'm not human, as you are—decay cannot touch my flesh, as it will touch yours in time. But he imprisoned me in this land, where in time I'll be taken by the Shadow..."

"What is this Shadow?"

Golden eyes watched Elak, luminous in the glow. "You saw it as a man's shadow—eh? A man such as yourself? But I saw it as Solonala's shadow. Every being sees the Shadow as his own. For it is his own. It is the ultimate death. It is destruction. This land is its home, but it can come to other worlds when gateways have been opened."

Gateways—such as the pool in the Pikhts' underground den!

"And it is here that the gods come when they die, Elak." Her voice was hushed. "You heard them pass, I think. Darkness always comes when the dead gods go by, for they wander this lost land alone in eternal night..."

Faint infinitely far away, there sounded a thin murmur—the hum of a plucked harpstring. Dim and drowsy, it stole into Elak's mind until, scarcely aware he heard it, he realized that he was nodding sleepily. Solonala watched him alertly out of great golden eyes.

"I hear magic," she said.

The harpstring throbbed on, blanketing Elak in drowsiness. As he went down into slumber he was conscious of Solonala leaning toward him, cat-face puzzled...and then darkness...

He dreamed. He dreamed of the black galley's cabin and of Dalan, crouching over his crystal globe. Within the sphere a flame rose up like a blossoming flower. It grew and lifted till it towered above the Druid's glistening bald head.

Its scarlet tip bent down, expanded into a lambent rose of fire. It swayed and trembled in midair. Dalan prayed.

"Mider hear me. God of the Druids, Lord of Flame, let your hand draw back this man from the Shadow—".

The vision faded. The dim murmur of a harpstring put a period to it. Vaguely Elak saw Solonala's face swimming in silver mistiness, her lips parted.

Again the harp sent its sorcerous whispering into Elak's sleeping mind—Elf's harp, fraught with deadly magic!

"Elak!"

Dalan's voice!

The harpstring twanged angrily. Above its noise came a harsh cry.

"Elak! Mider aid me—Elak! Hear me!"

The tall adventurer sprang to full wakefulness, his hand racing to the dagger at his belt. A low murmuring sounded from without the cave. Elak got quietly to his feet and moved toward the portal.

There he paused, his eyes wide. On the flat rock before the cave mouth crouched Solonala, her white body gleaming in the shifting shadow-patterns, and all about her, genuflecting and abjecting themselves in ghastly worship, was a horde of tiny, hideous white things that moved so swiftly Elak could not clearly define their outlines. Indeed, he had no chance, for as he appeared Solonala lifted her head, saw him, and flung out a slim arm commandingly. The white beings streamed away and were lost in the distance.

Now Elak saw what had previously escaped him.

Towering to the sky beyond Solonala, menacing and terrible, loomed—the Shadow!

The girl let her arm drop to her side. Without moving she watched Elak.

"Elf's magic brought the Shadow here while you slept," she said. "I could not waken you, though I tried. Those little ones—I made them. Living things, to appease the Shadow's hunger while we flee. Perhaps we can escape." She paused doubtfully.

From empty air roared the voice of Dalan. "Courage, Elak! I come—and with aid!"

And the voice of Elf, disembodied, gentle-mocking. "What can Mider do against the Shadow, Druid? Your god lives—and there is no life in Ragnarok."

The immense Shadow on the horizon grew darker. The flickering patterns in the air seemed to weave faster, troubled.

Without warning Elak saw the Shadow fold down tremendously and swoop upon him. He felt Solonala's soft body shuddering against his, and his arms went instinctively about her. The faun-girl cried out—and her voice was clipped off into utter silence. Blackness abysmal and unearthly smothered them.

They were one with the Shadow. They were nothingness—annihilation, complete and final emptiness. And yet Elak was dreadfully conscious of a feeling of power—cosmic power, terrible in its illimitable vastness. Aside from this, nothing existed for him. Solonala's body no longer pressed against his. He felt the fortress of his soul, his mind, crumbling under the assault of the Shadow.

And, suddenly, hope came. How it first manifested itself Elak did not understand, but he realized that no longer was he being absorbed into the Shadow. Something was pulling him back—lifting him from the sucking void that was annihilation.

He heard the Druid's voice, strained, triumphant.

"Mider! Save him, Mider—god of oak and fire—"

Light flashed out all around—warm, rose-tinted, luminous flame. In its fierce glow was revealed the figure of Solonala, unearthly in her beauty—and also the incredible thing on which the two stood. It was a hand.

Eight-fingered, colossal, it was no earthly hand. The hand of Mider himself, reaching down into the hell of the Shadow at the Druid's prayer. The Titan hand swept upward, carrying Elak and Solonala...

It checked itself. Blackness crept back, dimming the rosy flame-walls. A sea of shadow rose like a tide, and the hand began to sink down, slowly at first, and then with ever-increasing speed.

Dalan's cry came, despairing, inarticulate. And Elf's soft laughter.

Solonala knelt beside Elak. She put her arms around his neck; tender lips brushed his. Then, before he could move, she sprang away and flung herself into the void. For an intolerable age-long second her white and gold figure loomed against blackness—and was gone. A cry, gull-plaintive, drifted to Elak's ears as he started forward.

He was too late. The hand of the god swept up. Elak fell to his knees, struggling to drag himself to where Solonala had vanished...and then there was only darkness around him, and the howling and shrieking of great winds...

CHAPTER EIGHT
They Come to Cyrena

"Elak." It was Lycon's voice.

Elak opened his eyes. Gray light bathed him.

He was in the corridor of the pool, in the underground Pikht temple. Above him hovered the small fat figure of Lycon, round face alight with anxiety.

"Are you alive, Elak? Did those damned dwarfs—"

Elak drew a long, deep breath, got painfully to his feet, water cascading from his hair and garments. He looked down to where, beside him, the surface of the sunken basin lay blue and calm, untroubled by the Shadow that had once darkened it.

"I've just dragged you from there," Lycon said, following his gaze. "You shot up from the water like a cork."

"There was no other?" Elak asked. "You saw no one else in the pool?"

Lycon was silent for a time, watching his friend's eyes. Presently he shook his head.

"No," he said softly. "There was no other."

And then there was no more talk for a while, because Velia led in the blood-smeared oarsmen, who had just slain the last of the Pikhts; and Lycon was noisy about the number of dwarfs he had cut down and was, he said, almost thirsty enough to drink water.

"But not quite," he added. "Let's get back to the galley. It wasn't damaged much by the storm, Elak, and we can launch it in two days…"

So again the black galley drove northward through the Inland Sea, skirting the western shores of Crenos Isle, on through the swirling waters until white cliffs loomed on the horizon. And there, when it was least expected, Duke Granicor's ship came down on them as the galley was beached.

"Mider rot him!" the Druid growled, climbing ponderously over the rail, his brown, sea-stained garment flapping in the wind. "There's no time to fight him now, Elak. We've got to get the chiefs together, lead them against the Northmen."

"My brother," Elak said. "Don't forget him."

"I know. But that must come later. You can't help Orander till the Vikings are driven from Elf's fortress, where they have their headquarters and where your brother's a prisoner."

Lycon swaggered up, a flagon swinging against his side. "By the Nine Hells and a dozen more," he observed, "are we afraid of Granicor? Go on ahead, Elak, and take Dalan with you. Give me two oarsmen and I'll stay here and—"

"You're drunk," Elak said without rancor. "Go away."

He turned to stare at the long galley that was rapidly growing larger as it swept shoreward. Elak's spirits had been dampened since his adventure with the Pikhts, and the image of Solonala could not be dimmed even by Velia's caresses. Her self-sacrifice had shaken him more than he knew. And within him had crystallized a burning desire to cross blades with Elf, to slay the warlock minstrel—and swiftly!

So he agreed with Dalan. "We'll head inland, eh?"

"To Sharn Forest. The chiefs will gather there, with their men. I've sent a messenger, and the word will go through Cyrena. When the armies have gathered at Sharn, we'll move north on Elf's fortress."

"Good! I wish I had my rapier, though—this sword's too heavy." Elak made the tempered blade hiss through the air, and Dalan chuckled.

"You can spill blood with it, though. Come. Granicor is almost within bowshot."

Dalan in the lead, the band set out to climb the white cliffs, reaching the summit as the Duke of Poseidonia beached his galley. Granicor wasted no time in threats; grimly silent, he led his crew in pursuit.

But the duke was soon left behind. This was familiar country to Dalan, and swiftly the party marched through a tangled forest wilderness, even Velia, touched by eagerness that enabled her to keep pace easily. That night they camped in a little valley by a stream that chuckled pleasantly as it wound among furze and bracken.

Elak, sitting by the fire, idly plaited Velia's bronze hair. "It's good to be in Cyrena again," he told her. "I never thought I'd walk this land again. Do you like it, Velia?"

She nodded, the firelight bronze on her face. "It's rough and wild and—and honest, somehow. Strong men must live here, Elak."

"The Northmen are stronger," Dalan growled. "At least, until Cyrena has a leader." He reached out a huge hand and retrieved Lycon, who was reeling dangerously close to the fire. "Bah, this drunken dog! But he's a faithful one, at least."

"Only the gods know my true worth," Lycon said surprisingly and collapsed in an inert heap, muttering faintly. Suddenly he sat up, his eyes bright. "Listen, Elak!"

As he spoke feet came trampling through the underbrush. Granicor's voice bellowed a raucous command. Yelling men charged down the slope.

"Gods!" Elak snapped. "He's trailed us, somehow. To arms!" His sharp cry cut icily through the night; swords gleamed redly; and the next moment Granicor and his crew were within the circle of firelight.

Dulled by the heat of the flames, not expecting attack, yet Dalan's men met the charge bravely. The two forces came together, crashed and mingled, and then it was a whirling fire lit madness of blood and steel. Granicor headed directly for Elak, and, nothing loath, the tall adventurer sprang to meet him, sword hissing. The blades shrieked together in midair, were sent flying by the power of the blows, and, weaponless, Elak and Granicor closed, the duke snarling oaths, the other watchful and silent. They went down, scattering embers from the fire's edge.

Suddenly a shrill, warning cry came, above a low thunder of hoofs that boomed out from near by.

"Vikings! 'Ware—*Vikings!* The Northmen!"

And down into the valley rode red-bearded giants, roaring, spears driving, swords hewing, driving resistlessly over the campfire as they had swept down on Cyrena. Men screamed and died beneath trampling hoofs, and those who lived fled into the forest. In a moment the encampment was empty, save for the Northmen, the dead, and two men who lay locked in furious struggle on the ground.

Elak's arm was locked about Granicor's throat, but the duke's bull-thewed legs were slowly crushing his ribs, forcing the breath from his body, when the Vikings prodded the two apart with ungentle blades.

"Thunder of Thor!" a harsh voice grunted. "What madmen are these? Guthrum, they—"

Guthrum! At that name Elak tore free, sprang to his feet, heedless of the steel points that pricked him. His stare found a red-bearded giant in chain mail and brimless helmet, a man whose face had once been strong and powerful and valorous—a man whose eyes were dead!

Blue eyes, dull and cold and bitterly ferocious, watched Elak. This was Guthrum, leader of the Northmen, whose pact with Elf had resulted in the imprisonment of Orander, King of Cyrena.

"Guthrum?" It was Granicor's voice. "The Viking? My people aren't at war with yours. I am from Poseidonia!" The duke stood squarely facing Guthrum, looking up defiantly at the somber figure on horseback.

Without replying the Northman lashed out with a mail-shod foot, sent it driving into Granicor's face. Blood spurted as the duke reeled back. He caught himself, fumbled for a weapon that was not there—and hurled himself forward, up at Guthrum's throat, snarling a blazing oath.

The Viking's horse reared; Granicor went down under driving hoofs. Bitter laughter shook Guthrum, but the dull rage in his eyes was unchanged as he looked down on the prostrate Atlantean, turned to eye Elak. The tall adventurer felt a shudder course down his spine as he met that dreadful blue gaze. Something had been drained from the Viking chief, and there sat in his eyes that which was not human.

Granicor staggered upright, and Guthrum wheeled his mount to face the gory figure. In silence he listened while the duke choked out furious curses born of agonizing rage and shame. And then: "Do you think I fear such as you? Do you think I fear anything on Earth—after what a warlock has shown me?" The dull stare of the Viking was utterly horrible in its cold ferocity. "I, who have come sane from the vaults of Elf's citadel—shall I fear your curses?"

He clapped spurs to his horse, went thundering into the darkness. From the gloom his voice came roaring back: *"Crucify those men!"*

CHAPTER NINE
The Chiefs in Sharn

Spurred by the menace of Guthrum's words, Elak tore free momentarily from his captors, but as he turned to the forest they were upon him. He fought furiously, desperately—uselessly. He was born down, held powerless in the grip of red-bearded, mail-clad giants, as Granicor, his face a bloody ruin, was also held.

Working swiftly, the Vikings stripped Granicor of his armor, dragged him to where a great oak grew nearby. He cursed them, striving to break away, his tiny eyes flaming with rage and fear. But thongs lifted the duke's apelike body, binding him inexorably against the tree's bole. His arms were drawn up behind him, circling the trunk—and with iron spikes and improvised hammers the Northmen went about their crimson work.

Elak watched, white-faced, as iron tore through flesh and bone, listening to the frightful cries that burst through Granicor's mangled lips. The Vikings left him at last, letting him hang by his hands, shoulders wrenched almost out of their sockets. They turned to Elak.

He tensed for a hopeless struggle. And abruptly he sensed astonishment in the craggy faces about him. The Vikings had turned, staring, to where a gross brown figure stood just within the circle of firelight.

Dalan—his toad face hideous with fury, huge hands lifted. He made no sound, but so dreadful was the menace in his expression that the Northmen were held motionless for a moment. Then a cry went up; they surged forward, blades ready.

The Druid flung out his arms in a strange gesture—as though he hurled a curse at his enemies. From his thick lips a word came, unfamiliar, alien. There was power in the gesture, power in the word Dalan spoke. The air seemed to quiver, charged with electric force.

Thunder burst in Elak's ears. He was flung back, blinded by a sheet of white flame that washed the clearing in stark brilliance. For a second he lost consciousness.

Then the Druid was lifting him, muttering curses. Feebly Elak freed himself, stared around. The place looked as though lightning had struck it. The grass and trees were seared and blackened, and of the Northmen only charred corpses in half-melted armor remained.

"Ishtar!" Elak whispered, his voice unsteady. "What—what happened, Dalan? Is this more of your—magic?"

The Druid nodded. "A fire-magic I cannot work often. We have power over flame, Elak—and there's flame in the sky as well as on earth. With Mider's aid, I drew down the lightning. Those barbarians died by their god's thunderbolt." Vicious laughter shook the huge bulk. "Lucky for you I wasn't cut down when the Vikings rode in. Look, their horses have stampeded—those that aren't blasted to death."

Elak touched his singed eyebrows. "I don't see how I escaped. Can you direct this wizard lightning of yours, Dalan?"

"Perhaps. Also the Northmen wore armor, and you have none. That may have accounted for it. See—the man they crucified, Granicor—he wears no armor, and he's still alive. Barely, I think."

Elak's gaze went to where the tortured body of the duke hung from the oak. He hesitated, then went forward purposefully.

"Lycon?" he asked over his shoulder. "Velia? Are they safe?"

The Druid nodded. "Yes, they're waiting not far away. But the rest of the crew are dead or scattered. We'll have to move quickly to reach Sharn Forest—I didn't know the Vikings had come this far south, and four of us can't very well fight an army. In Sharn we'll meet the chiefs—what are you doing, you fool? Freeing that dog?"

"He's an Atlantean, at least," Elak said, wrenching at one of the iron spikes that transfixed Granicor's hand. "And this is no way for any man to die."

The duke had apparently lost consciousness. As the last spike came free, his body slumped down in a bloody huddle at the tree's foot. Elak paused.

"He can't live long. But I don't like to leave him here to be tortured by the Northmen if they come. Yet—"

"We can't take him with us! Gods, will you feed him and and nurse him after he's just tried to slit your throat—while Elf rules Cyrena and holds your brother captive. I tell you we must get to Sharn—and quickly!"

"Very well," Elak agreed, turning toward the forest. "He can't live till morning—no man could, with those wounds. To Sharn, then—and after that we march on Elf's fortress."

"We march on Guthrum's army," Dalan grunted. "Wherever it may be. But it won't be far from the warlock's citadel. Guthrum's headquarters is there."

His ungainly figure vanished in the shadows, Elak at his side. And at the foot of a great oak tree a frightful figure dragged itself half erect, an apelike man, seared and blood-stained and wounded on hands and feet. Mangled lips writhed and opened.

"Elf's—fortress," a harsh voice whispered, cracked with agony. *"And Guthrum!"* A gout of blood spewed from the man's throat and a paroxysm of coughing shook him. He clung to the oak, dragged himself upright, grinning with abysmal pain.

"So I won't live till morning?" he mumbled. "I'll live—till I find Guthrum!"

Duke Granicor staggered a few steps and collapsed, but he lay inert for only a moment. Then, very slowly, wheezing and groaning between clenched teeth, he began to drag himself into the forest...

Elak stood before the Druid altar in Sharn Forest, a great gray stone, its top hollowed out into a shallow basin that was stained darkly by countless ages of sacrifice. It was dawn. A day and a night had passed since the encounter with Granicor and the Northmen, and for a few hours Elak had slept in the shadow of the Druid stone, while the chiefs gathered, drawn to Sharn by swift messengers. Lycon and Velia had slept beside him, and Dalan had watched, greeting each newcomer as he arrived. Now nearly all the chiefs were here, a grim half-circle in the cold light of dawn, their strong faces betraying of their thoughts. Yet, somehow, Elak sensed hostility in the eyes watching him, and their gaze was suspicious as well as appraising. Dalan realized something of this, for his ugly face was set in an appalling snarl.

A young chieftain pushed forward, bull-necked, ruddy-cheeked. He advanced till he stood only a few feet from Dalan and halted with folded arms.

"Have I your leave to speak, Druid?" he asked mockingly.

Somber eyes watched him. "Ay, Halmer. Since Cyrena chooses a cub for spokesman—speak."

Halmer's laugh was scornful. "My words are those of all, I think. Well—listen, then. The Northmen are still on the coasts. They will not come south. If they do, we can drive them back."

"What of Orander?" Dalan asked. "What of your king?"

The young chief hesitated. Then, gathering courage from the Druid's calm, he snapped, "We'll fight for our own holdings, if need be. But Elf's magic—who can fight that? I say, let the Northmen hold the coast, if they want it. They've not troubled my lands yet. If they do, I'll know how to drive them away."

"And one by one you will go down beneath Guthrum," Dalan said. "Halmer speaks for you all? You'll let your king rot in Elf's power, you'll let the Northmen hang like a cankerous sore on the coast—Mider! but you need a king's strong hand to rule you! Without Orander you squabble among yourselves like a pack of snarling curs."

Some looked shamefaced at that, but none spoke.

Finally: "Who is this Elak?" one asked. "You say he's Zeulas, the king's brother. Perhaps. But you ask us to bow down before a man who killed his stepfather—a man who may, then, kill his brother and rule Cyrena!"

Elak growled a curse. He pushed past the Druid.

"It wouldn't take much of a man to rule you, I think," he snapped harshly. "There were not so many fools and cowards here when I left Cyrena. I killed Norian, yes—but in fair fight, and most of you remember that my stepfather had no great love for either Orander or me. But as for my wanting to rule this land of women—bah! I've asked your aid. If you won't give it, I'll go to Elf's fortress alone and find my brother."

At his words there was a stir. One man, a tall, lean oldster in dented armor, came to cast his sword at Elak's feet.

"Well, I'll go with you, at least," he said. "And my followers are not few. I remember you in the old days, Zeulas—and I know you speak true words now."

With antique courtesy Elak gravely retrieved the fallen sword, touched his forehead with the hilt, and returned it to the oldster.

"Thanks, Hira. I remember you, too, and that you were always ready to fight for Cyrena. These other dogs—"

Hira's lean face twisted wryly. "No, Zeulas—or Elak. They are not dogs; they're brave men all—but fear of Elf's magic and hatred of each other have made them less noble."

Brawny Halmer laughed. "Go with Hira, stranger—and you too, Druid, since he's a madman too. I go back to my own holding now—and send me no more messengers." He turned on his heel, to be halted by the curt voice of Dalan.

"Wait."

He turned. "Well?"

"You fight among yourselves, you follow cubs like Halmer—and you fear Elf's magic. Now for ages on uncountable ages the Druids have dwelt in Cyrena, and they will not go down now before the gods of the North—not for the lack of a few strong sword arms. So I tell you this: Druid magic may protect you against Elf's wizardries. And it may not. But, by Mider...!" The toad face was a venomous devil mask; Dalan spat the words at the chiefs, "...by Mider Elf won't protect you against the power of the Druids! And we have not lost our power!"

Some shrank back, and there were pale faces among those turned to Dalan. But Halmer laughed scornfully shrugging broad shoulders.

"Old men and children may fear you," he mocked, "but I do not."

The Druid lifted a huge hand, pointed upward. His voice came sonorously, laden with menace.

"Then listen, Halmer. And—watch! Should it not be dawn now?"

At his words a little movement of apprehension shook the chiefs. None had noticed before, but over the brightening vault of the sky an iron-gray cope of cloud had been drawn. Heavily it lay above Sharn, growing darker as they watched. A shadow fell on the clearing. The trees loomed strangely ominous in the dimness.

Yet Halmer laughed again. "Do we fear clouds? Your magic is feeble—charlatan!"

Dalan said nothing; his black eyes, half hidden by sagging lids, watched Halmer. A cold wind blew through Sharn; whispers rustled the forest. Steadily it grew darker.

From the chiefs a low murmur of fear went up.

Elak felt Velia creep close to him, put his arm protectingly about her slim waist. For once Lycon was silent, looking up apprehensively. Before the altar Dalan's misshapen figure towered, arms raised in menace.

Halmer's voice was not quite steady, his face a little less ruddy, as he barked, "I'll not stay here longer, I—"

"Go," the Druid said, "if you dare."

Halmer clapped hand to sword, turned, pushed through the group of chiefs. None followed as he moved to the edge of the clearing. Then, about to step into the dark shadows beneath the trees, he paused and drew back a step.

It seemed to Elak that, far in the gloom, something was watching—something infinitely horrible, avid for prey. And Halmer must have sensed something of this. He wavered, without taking a step forward or back.

"Druid magic is feeble," Dalan whispered. "What holds you, Halmer? There is nothing in the wood."

Nothing—but a soft coughing, a nameless rustle in primeval, shadow-darkened forest. The dark dawn lowered over Sharn.

"Old men and children fear me," the Druid mocked. "But you do not, Halmer. No."

Snarling a furious curse, the young chief leaped forward into the gloom as though casting off unseen shackles. The murmuring deepened, grew to a low, sullen roar. Halmer was a dim shadow plunging forward between towering trunks.

Men saw him pause, casting a startled glance upward.

His sword flashed out—and the roar of the forest grew deafening. From above something came hurtling down, a great branch, torn from its parent tree, sent plunging through foliage upon a man who screamed once in frantic fear and died. Men saw Halmer borne down, broken, under the terrible impact. The roaring died to a faint murmur, lessened almost to nothing.

"Druid magic is feeble," Dalan said softly. "Does Halmer think that now?" He swung to face the chiefs, bellowing. "Follow Halmer if you dare! Leave Sharn without swearing fealty to Elak—and you walk the forests under the Druid curse. By Mider! Go—and see how long you live!"

But none dared face the Druid's wrath. One by one the chiefs came forward and cast their blades before Elak.

So Elak took command of Cyrena's armies—and from Sharn Forest the word went forth like flame: Gather! Sharpen steel! The land is risen against the Northmen—and the king's brother leads Cyrena against Elf and Guthrum!

Gather! Gather to march against the Viking hordes!

CHAPTER TEN
In the Valley of Skulls

Lycon swilled wine from a goatskin, set it down, and wiped his mouth with the back of a pudgy hand. His sharp eyes drifted over serried ranks of armored men, flashing steel, horses snorting hungry for battle; it had taken twelve days to draw the last fighting man from the mountains and far places of Cyrena; three days more of steady marching to reach the Valley of Skulls, named for a bandit who, long ago, had littered the slopes with the heads of his enemies. But the Northmen had drawn together swiftly and had made their stand, too, in the Valley of Skulls. A river separated the two armies, safely beyond bowshot of each other.

"When do we attack?" Lycon asked Elak, who stood beside him on a little knoll.

"Soon," the lean adventurer said, "the sun will rise in a few minutes. At sunrise we cross Monra River." He tested the metal of his rapier. "It's good to have a weapon like this again. I'll give this blade its baptism today."

"And I'll give mine," Velia broke in, coming lightly up the hill toward them. Her slim armor-clad body gleamed in the gray light of false dawn. Her bronze hair foamed out from a helmet that was too small to prison its bright masses. "This is different from Poseidonia, Elak. This was the life I was meant for—not a perfumed harem in Granicor's palace."

"Yes, it's different from Poseidonia," Lycon said glumly. "They have good liquor there. It's next to impossible to get wine in this barbarian land, and the bitter ale your countrymen drink is too much for me, Elak. Gall and wormwood!" He spat and reached for the goatskin again.

Elak drew Velia close to him, kissed her swiftly. "We may meet death today," he told the flushed girl. "I'd rather you'd stay in camp."

Velia smiled and shook her head. "I've tasted war, and I like the draft. Listen!"

Far along the valley trumpets blew a call; they grew louder, closer, till the tocsin resounded from slope to slope. Across the river the armies of the Northmen waited...

"They mean to use arrows as we cross," Elak said. "But I think they'll be disappointed. My plans are made."

Trumpets shouted, drums groaned, banners lifted, streaming in the chill dawn wind, and the army of Cyrena moved forward. Brawny, fair-skinned, yellow-haired warriors, following their chiefs, riding their chargers into the foaming current of Monra River—and watching, Elak smiled.

"Hira and Dalan have led men to the Vikings' flanks," he told Velia. "The Northmen think we'll ford the river near the center of their front. But—look!"

The first rank of Elak's army were in the river, dashing across in the face of a storm of arrows. On the opposite bank waited pikemen, and behind them, armored red-beards with swords and axes. The men of Cyrena seemed suddenly to surge forward in the wake of the advance guard, hurling themselves toward Monra River, down the valley's slope. But in their rear ranks a concerted movement was taking place; whole troops and companies were racing to left and right, slanting toward the river, attempting to outflank the Northmen.

"What's this?" Velia asked. "The Vikings can ride as fast as our men. Why—"

Across the river the enemy had seen Elak's move, and their flanks moved outward—but not far. A great shout arose far to the left, and, a moment later, a thunderous roar came from the right. Over the ridge, on both wings of the

Viking army, rode warriors, streaming down the slopes, swords and lances gleaming in the sunlight.

"Hira—and Dalan!" Lycon said. "They outflanked the Northmen in the night. They'll give us a chance to cross Monra."

Now the strategy was evident; a thin line of warriors held the bank of the river, their bowmen keeping the enemy engaged. And the rear ranks of Cyrena galloped to left and right, racing into Monra River, plunging across it and up the steep shores in the face of a hail of arrows and steel. They could not have succeeded had it not been for Hira and Dalan, whose warriors spread ruin and confusion in the Viking flanks.

"We've crossed," Elak barked, eyes agleam. "Now we're on equal ground—it's strength, not strategy, that counts now we've crossed Monra. Come on!" He turned to a great white charger that stood nearby, stamping his impatience, his hoofs striking fire from the rocks underfoot. With one leap Elak was in the saddle.

Upright in the stirrups, shouting, rapier unsheathed, he thundered down the slope, and behind him rode Lycon and Velia—down to the water's edge, into Monra River, foam splashing high as they charged across. A roar went up from the warriors—and the next moment, driven back by the impetus of Elak's forces, slashing and thrusting at his heels, the Northmen gave way up the slope, desperately contesting each inch of ground lost

Then there was nothing but a red maelstrom of hewing and cutting, ax and sword and strongly driven spear; screaming of horses that galloped by with riders clinging with one hand and warring with the other; horses plunging and dying in a welter of thunderous crimson ruin—giant men fighting and falling and slaying as they fell.

Raven banners toppled. Shouts of *"Odin! Thor with us!"* mingled with roars of *"Cyrena! Cyrena!"* Elak thrust and thrust again, guiding his steed with one hand as it stumbled and leaped over knots of prostrate, struggling men and still, bloody bodies. Above the ranks that surrounded him he saw the Druid's head nodding and swaying far to the right, and a great sword hewed steadily about Dalan, cutting a wide swath of corpses. And ahead, in the front rank of the Viking army, rode Guthrum, red beard flaming, moving like a towering pestilence among men whose helms and heads were crushed by his bloody ax.

"Thor! Thor with us!"

"Cyrena!"

Sweat and blood smeared Elak's face. He tried to find Lycon and Velia, but knew it was impossible in the melee. A Viking rode at him yelling, spear leveled; the white warhorse leaped forward and aside at Elak's urging. The spearpoint grazed his cheek as he swayed aside, and his blade sank deep into the Northman's hairy throat. He whipped it out, steel singing, and thrust at a new foe.

The sun rose higher, and the reek of spilled gore mingled with the stench of sweat. At the top of the ridge the Vikings rallied, knowing that if they were driven past it they were lost. And like a massacre King Guthrum raged among his enemies, his ax rising and falling steadily, rhythmically, dreadful as the hammer of the Northmen's god Thor. The army of Cyrena was checked—driven back a little down the slope.

"Forward!" Elak spurred his charger, sent it leaping against the mad horde that swept down Skull Valley.

"Cyrena! Ho, Cyrena!" His rapier darted out like a snake striking, and its touch was as deadly. A Viking fell, screaming his death cry.

And Elak's voice caught his army as it hesitated on the brink of retreat that led to destruction. One man, mad with valor, facing an army—and then Cyrena held, held and resisted and charged to meet the Northmen as they poured down.

"Slay!" A voice screamed—Dalan's hoarse, trumpet-loud. "Slay the Vikings! For Cyrena!"

Men dazed and exhausted with battle felt new life pulse within them; blood-drunken, murder-hungry, they flooded against their enemies in a blasting charge that could have only one result. Fighting bitterly, insanely, hopelessly, the Northmen were overwhelmed, pushed up to the crest—beyond it, down the slope, while from the Valley of Skulls the armies of Cyrena came like a consuming flame. It was the day of doom for the Vikings—their Ragnorok—and the raven banners fell in the dust and were trampled by racing hoofs.

"Slay! Slay the Vikings!"

Upright in his stirrups Elak shouted, seeing in the defeat of the Northmen the ruin of Guthrum, the end of Elf—the freeing of his brother Orander. Cyrena had conquered—that he knew. Beside him Lycon reined up, his round face flushed and bleeding.

"Ho, Elak! They run like rabbits!" Even now Lycon could not refrain from his habitual exaggeration. For the red-bearded giants were not fleeing; they fought on, hopelessly, slaying as they died.

Resolution flared in Elak's eyes. "Lycon—stay here. Lead our men." He whirled his horse.

"Where are you going, Elak?"

"To Elf's fortress! Now! I'll take him by surprise—"

The rest was lost as Elak clapped spurs down, galloped up to the ridge—along it, skirting the edge of the battle. Lycon's shout was unheard in the roar.

But another had seen Elak's flight. A horse broke from the uproar, raced in pursuit. Astride it sat Dalan, brown robe streaming. Not even in this battle had he donned armor, and strangely no weapon had touched him. But few could venture alive within the deadly sweep of the Druid's sword. The runes carved on its blade ran red now, dripping along the horse's flank as it raced after Elak.

And behind them rose the death cry of the Vikings in Cyrena, while after Elak, after the Druid, rode vengeance. Guthrum on his huge black charger, grimly silent, leading a little band of Northmen—and there was cold murder in the Viking king's bitter eyes!

CHAPTER ELEVEN
How Granicor Died

Elf's fortress rose, a great grim castle of stone, flanked by the sullen waters of the Inland Sea. It was empty now, or nearly so, for the Vikings had gone to meet Elak's army in the Valley of Skulls, and Elf kept few servitors. Men whispered that not all of these were human.

In the dimness of early morning a man had come down from the hills and entered the citadel, hoisting himself painfully from stone to jagged stone of the wall that guarded Elf's privacy. But the rivet-studded, iron barbican that blocked the inner gate he could not pass; and so he waited, skulking in the shadows, caressing the edge of a long sword he carried in one maimed hand. The face of Duke Granicor was like that of one of the gargoyles that grinned from the roofs of the fortress. Incredibly he had lived, had made his way north in search of Guthrum, and now, knowing nothing of the battle in the Valley of the Skulls, he sat on his haunches, a malignant fire glowing in his eyes. His clothing was in rags, and he more than ever resembled some monstrous shaggy ape lying in wait for its prey.

The sun was high when at last he heard the clatter of hoofs and swiftly drew back into a shadowy niche. Elak and the Druid reined to a halt before the door of iron let into the outer wall, and the tall adventurer swung from his horse, his gaze examining the rough stones. The other's voice halted him.

"Wait, Elak. We won't have to climb. I'll open this door for you."

Dalan, without dismounting, reached into the folds of his robe, drew forth something which he hurled at the barrier. Immediately a sheet of blinding white flame sprang up, hiding the wall momentarily, setting the horses lunging and prancing in terror. Elak was nearly jerked from his feet as he fought to hold his steed.

Then the flames died. Where the door had been was a white-hot puddle of melted iron, and the stones of the portal were blackened and cracked by the intense heat. The Druid spurred forward his horse, and it hurdled the searing liquid iron easily. Elak followed, just in time to see fire burst out from the grill of the barbican.

"So far, so good," Dalan grunted, watching the iron melt and drip to the stones of the courtyard. "But Elf doesn't depend on doors and walls alone."

Elak, looking up, did not answer. On the summit of the inner wall a gargoylish figure was carved seemingly of rugose dark stone, a creature that might have sprung from any of the Nine Hells. Stunted and huge and hideous it seemed to crouch above the courtyard, glaring down menacingly. Wide wings swept out from its gnarled shoulders. Somehow Elak sensed evil in the posture of the thing, the tiny eyes that seemed to watch him.

"Come! The barbican's down—"

The Druid's black warhorse stepped forward—and simultaneously Elak caught a flicker of movement from above, sensed rather than saw a great figure that hurtled down, wings sweeping, talons clutching murderously. He clapped spurs into the stallion, sent him driving against Dalan's steed. With the same movement he unsheathed his rapier, thrust up almost without aim.

A flapping of wings buffeted him. The weapon was torn from his grasp, and he crashed down on the stones, battling for his life with a monster that clawed and bellowed and ripped with vicious tusks—the thing he had thought carved from stone, the gargoyle, brought to evil life by Elf's dark sorcery. Exhausted as he was, Elak was no match for the creature. The fangs drove toward his throat; a foul breath was strong in his nostrils.

Then the weight on Elak's body was gone; gasping for breath, he saw the monster gripped by the Druid, lifted above the bald, gleaming head. There was tremendous strength in Dalan's gross frame. He crushed the struggling monster down on the flags, leaped on it with crushing feet. His sword swung redly...

"By Bel," Elak murmured, retrieving his rapier. "Is that a devil? I've never seen beast or man like that before, Dalan."

"Nor has anyone else," the Druid informed him, staring down at the monster's still body. "It's an elemental, and devil's a good name for it. Elf set it to guard the gate. Well..." He swung his blade. "...if I can cut through the warlock's neck as easily—good! Leave your horse, Elak. We must go on foot from here."

Hidden in a niche nearby, Duke Granicor watched, wondering. But when Dalan and Elak passed the threshold, vanishing from sight in the depths of the fortress, Granicor sprang out and followed them.

And down from the hills rode a half-dozen horsemen, led by King Guthrum, spurring and yelling as they galloped. Only the Viking chief was silent, gripping his war-ax on which the blood had dried in dark red splashes...

"To the vaults," Dalan said, hurrying swiftly along empty stone corridors. "I know the way. I've seen it often in my crystal. Hurry!" The Druid almost seemed to sense the danger that followed at their heels.

Elak's quick gaze searched the depths of side passages that led into enigmatic depths of the fortress. They raced on, through high-vaulted tunnels, down winding stairs dimly lit or in darkness, across great rooms that housed the magnificence of a king's palace.

They met no one. The vast citadel was deserted, or seemed so. And at last, when Elak guessed they had penetrated far underground, they came to a metal door, strangely figured with cabalistical signs, before which Dalan paused.

"This is the heart of Elf's castle," he said softly. "Here he holds your brother captive. Elak—" The Druid fumbled under his robe, drew out a long object wrapped in cloth. He unwound the casing, revealing a short dagger apparently carved out of crystal.

"There is strong magic in this," Dalan said, handing the weapon, hilt first, to Elak. "And it will slay the warlock where no earthly steel can spill his blood. It is the Druid knife of sacrifice."

Nodding, Elak slipped it into his belt. Dalan turned to the metal door, pushed it open. A flame of amber light blinded the two momentarily. Then their vision cleared; they stepped across the threshold...

They stood on a platform that thrust out from a wall of sheer rock that towered up and to both sides and down into a fathomless immensity of golden blaze that hurt the eyes with its fires. Ahead they saw nothing but clouds—amber clouds billowing and shifting continually, drifting like the sea all about them; flame-bright, yet cool as fog in its clinging mistiness. Elak shrank back involuntarily before the strangeness of the spectacle.

"Steady!" The Druid's huge hand gripped him. "Steady, now. We've a perilous road here—watch!"

Something swam into view from the mists to the left, a black object that seemed like a huge flat-topped globe as it slipped silently closer. Hanging unsupported in the amber fog it emerged, drifting forward until it hung not a foot from the edge of the platform on which the two men stood. Now Elak saw that it was indeed a globe, like an orange with its top sliced off, hollowed out into a great cup.

"We ride that chariot!" Dalan whispered. "Follow me."

He lumbered forward a few steps and sprang. The brown-robed, gross figure hurtled above the golden depths, plunged down safely within the hollow globe. It did not even sway beneath the impact.

"Elak!" The Druid had turned, was beckoning. "Hurry!"

The tall adventurer dared give himself no time to think; he leaped, his heart hammering. Almost he overshot the mark, but Dalan's hands clutched him, lifting him to safety. White-faced, Elak stood erect on legs that were not quite steady.

The rim of the globe was waist-high. The diameter of the circular floor was about four feet, made of some unfamiliar jet-black substance he did not recognize.

The weird chariot swung in its orbit, skirting bare rock walls. The platform from which they had leaped was lost in the golden haze. They drifted through an endless sea of cool fire...

As Granicor followed Dalan and Elak through the fortress he had soon come to realize that he, too, was being followed in his turn. Not guessing that the man he sought was among those who pursued him, he pressed on more swiftly—and the metal door that led to the platform above the abyss swung open under his hand as Elak leaped to the hollow globe. Guthrum stared in astonishment, not realizing until the black sphere had been lost in the mists that the noise of his pursuers was growing louder. Then he stepped across the threshold and flattened himself against the rock wall, sword lifted.

Thus Guthrum's men did not at first see the duke. They came in a mob through the doorway, yelling like wolves. One nearly went over the platform's edge as he twisted in midair, trying to halt his plunging rush. He reeled against a companion, clutching his shoulder—and neither one of them saw their slayer!

For Granicor lunged forward roaring. The sweep of his great sword toppled one Viking against the other, and they went over the brink in a flurry of arms and legs and a knife-edged shriek of despair. Before the other Northmen knew death was among them Granicor had struck again, shouting as he caught sight of Guthrum's hated face. A helmet was crushed like paper, and bone shattered under the rush of the duke's steel; then blades licked out, and a cry went up from the Vikings. Three had died already—and there were more to die that day.

For Granicor moved like a pestilence, iron muscles in his great-thewed body toughened by his hatred of King Guthrum. His brand fell and swung and murdered in a crash of ringing steel there above the golden abysses, and though he was unarmored, no thrust or cut seemed to have power to hurt him. Three he killed, and was wounded in breast and back and thigh. Blood gushed out through his tattered rags. Then even the hardy Vikings felt a shudder of horror go through them, for this madman, his body warped with torture, wounded almost to death—*laughed!* Granicor shouted with laughter, the insane glee that rose resistlessly within him as he cut his way toward Guthrum. Blood gushed from the half-healed wounds on hands and feet, mingling with the crimson welter that flooded the platform.

One man's head leaped from his shoulders; and on the backsweep of the sword Granicor drove steel deep into a Viking's side, slicing through chain mail like cardboard. He dashed blood and sweat from his eyes with a shapeless paw— saw one giant figure before him, a huge redbeard whose ax was driving down, screaming through cleft air. The duke leaped in, blade slashing.

The ax bit deep into Granicor's back. He shouted, stiffened. The sword dropped from his hands. In the bitter eyes of Guthrum a black laughter rose.

But the duke was not yet dead. He swayed, face contorted, clawing emptiness. He looked up and saw Guthrum standing alone above corpses, the only Northman left alive.

Roaring, he sprang.

Steel fingers locked in Guthrum's hairy throat. Weaponless, Granicor made of his body a human projectile that drove the red-bearded giant back and down—back to the platform's edge—and beyond!

The two men plunged into the abyss, locked in a death grip, Duke Granicor shouting mad triumph.

But from the Viking king came no sound as he fell through the golden mists to death.

CHAPTER TWELVE
Warlock and Druid

Swinging through empty space went the hollow globe with Elak and Dalan within it, on and on in a great curve till at last something loomed out of the dimness ahead. The Druid drew in his breath sharply.

"Leap after me, Elak—and swiftly."

A pinnacle, a tower, a jagged eidolon of granite swam into view, lifting from amber fog-clouds. Dalan climbed laboriously on the sloping, waist-high rim, crouching there. The steep crag drifted closer. And the Druid sprang—scrabbled with hand and foot to cling to the dangerously angled rock. Elak followed, knowing a sickening instant of cold horror as he felt beneath him incredible depths of emptiness. Then they stood together on the slope—and Dalan pointed to a tunnel mouth just above them.

"There's our road, Elak. Come."

They stumbled cautiously toward the cryptic opening in the rocks. It led to a short tunnel leading downward, very dimly lighted by the amber glow that filtered from the mouth. At the end of the passage was a door. It was unlocked; Dalan swung it open. Just beyond the threshold, on the rock floor, was a lamp, its bright flame illuminating every detail of the cave that lay before them.

It was empty save for a small square altar of dark stone and the figure of a man who knelt before it, staring into the coldly yellow depths of a jewel he clasped in stiff hands.

"Orander!" Elak almost shouted.

There was no answer.

Orander of Cyrena, Elak's brother, knelt as though carved from stone, his intent gaze riveted upon the jewel he gripped. He was younger than Elak, yet, somehow, he seemed older. Golden hair, unbound, grew in a leonine mane over the well-shaped head. There was strength in the king's face—power, and something of nobility.

But the man was—*veiled!*

Over his features there lay, like the shadow of death, an impalpable darkness, intangible, yet conveying a definite air of withdrawal. It seemed to Elak that, strangely, his brother was very far away, though his body was only a few feet distant. And even as he called again he knew that Orander would not hear.

"The king is lost to Cyrena," Dalan said quietly. "There is strong sorcery in the yellow jewel."

"I'll waken him, then," Elak grunted, moving forward. Suddenly he paused. Amazement flooded his lean face. For a second he seemed to strive futilely against empty air. His hands went out, seeming to slide across an invisible wall that blocked his way.

"Strong sorcery!" the Druid said. "No—don't use your rapier. You'd shatter it. There's only one way to reach Orander—and it's a perilous one."

At Elak's impatient gesture Dalan turned to the lamp. Swiftly he extinguished it and shut the door so that the yellow glow could not filter in. Intense blackness darkened the cave.

"There's only one road by which we can reach the king, Elak—a road I've never traveled. Watch."

Elak obeyed. He could see nothing. Flashing light-images played before his pupils, but gradually these faded and vanished. They were alone in darkness.

Then he saw a tiny pinpoint of yellow light.

"Do you see it?" Dalan muttered. Elak grunted assent. "Then follow it. Keep the light constantly before your eyes. Walk forward slowly until—until—"

The Druid's voice faded oddly and was lost in silence. Without hesitation Elak stepped toward the tiny yellow light. He expected to crash into the invisible barrier that had blocked his path, but it did not materialize. After he had advanced a dozen paces he paused. Orander should now be almost at his side.

Urgently came Dalan's hoarse voice. "Go on! Quickly!" The yellow light had vanished. For a moment Elak searched for it vainly; then, dimly, he saw it, winking like a tiny star. He moved on again, and as he did the light grew brighter.

Yet it was only a pinpoint, guiding him through utter blackness. As he went on he realized that he had traversed the length of the cave and should crash against the rock wall. Yet he did not. And the rock beneath his feet had a different feel—softer, more elastic.

Suddenly there was a moment of frightful vertigo, a wrenching jar that tore at every atom of his body. He felt utterly disoriented—strangely lost, curiously conscious of movement he could not analyze.

The darkness fled away and was gone. Cool yellow light was all around him. At Elak's side was the Druid—but no longer were they in the cave.

They stood on a glowing plain of amber, under a golden sky that was sunless and luminous. All around them was a featureless, coldly blazing expanse, stretching endlessly into infinity.

"Ishtar!" Elak's voice was hushed. "Where are we, Dalan? This isn't—Earth."

"No. We are in a far place now, and a dangerous one. We passed through a door into another world."

"A door?"

"The yellow jewel," Dalan said, "it is the bridge between our land and this world. More than that—"

The Druid broke off, staring. The distant glowing plains seemed to be undergoing an incredible transformation—lifting, rising like great waves, marching forward from the horizons toward the two men.

Elak caught a glimpse of Dalan's face, startled and apprehensive, and then the two were jerked apart. A gap widened in the earth between them. Elak caught a flashing glimpse of abysmal depths where red-orange fire glowed. He seemed to be spinning through empty space, rocketing across the great plain with furious speed. Briefly the world seemed to close about him, as though he was being crushed between the vast plains, which had somehow been folded in around him. He clutched his rapier hilt in hopeless desperation.

And then he stood alone on the great shining plain.

Nothing else was visible but the brazen amber sky; the Druid had vanished. It was utterly silent.

"Elak," a soft voice called. The tall adventurer turned. He saw no one.

Then, from empty air, there sprang—a shadow!

Two-dimensional, unreal, it grew darker, took on form and substance. As Elak gazed, a man grew into visibility and stood watching him, a slim, blue-eyed youth with soft flaxen hair. He wore a doeskin tunic, his only weapon a dirk girded at his belt. In his hand he gripped a harp.

Elak remembered the face he had seen in Dalan's crystal globe on the galley—the face of Elf the warlock, the same on which he looked now. And again he sensed the ageless, incredible evil that lurked in the depths of the candid blue eyes, watching as a devil might peer through a mask.

"I am Elf," the warlock said. "But I think you know that." He did not move as Elak unsheathed his rapier crouching menacingly, one foot forward.

"Yes, I know it," the tall adventurer answered warily.

"Where's Dalan? Bring him here—or I'll let blood flow from your throat before you can move to cast a spell."

Elf smiled. "No, my business is with you. Elak—you have spoiled my plans. But I have no wish to kill you. Instead, I'd rather see you on the throne of Cyrena."

"Eh?" Elak did not lower his blade. "What are you trying now? Bring Dalan here, I say!"

"Dalan has lied to you. He said I had your brother captive—"

"And I saw him! Your lies won't help."

"He's here, yes," Elf admitted. "But not a captive. In Cyrena he was a king. But in this land of mine he is more. I have made him—a god!"

"What are you talking about?" Elak snapped. "You're playing for time. Bring—"

The warlock swept his hand over the harp's strings. Throbbing sweetness, with a poignant undertone of bitterness rang out. Instantly they were in utter blackness.

And at that moment Elak thrust with his rapier, thrust at empty air. Cursing, he slashed blindly about. Suddenly the darkness lifted.

For an instant Elak saw his brother's face hovering gigantically above him, the weird veil of alienage still shrouding the strong features. In the king's eyes Elak saw withdrawal—a withdrawal so awe-inspiring that he felt momentarily cold, as though some breath of the unknown had touched him.

The voice of Elf came softly. "I have shown you Orander," the warlock murmured. "Now I shall show you more. You shall see the worlds over which the god who is Orander rules."

Again the dark veil fell.

Great vistas of flashing light, orange, scarlet, yellow, glittering with amazing beauty, down which fled Cyclopean shadows. Slowly the vision faded and became distinct. Elak seemed to be hovering in empty air above a huge city, many-tiered and gardened, that rose on the summit of a mountain beneath him.

Fantastic splendor ruled the city. Shining domes and minarets rose high above the wide marble streets, and arches and bridges spanned the lakes and canals where water—glowing with yellow radiance—moved sluggishly between its banks. The inhabitants of the city were not human.

They were beasts—and yet more than beasts. Elak was reminded of giant colossi of stone, winged monsters, bearded and talc-winged, lion-bodied, sleekly beautiful. Smoothly powerful muscles rolled beneath the satin pelts. And wise, wise and ancient beyond all imagination, were the faces that Elak saw. The plumes of the varicolored wings fluttered in the gentle breeze that swept over the mountaintop, honeysweet, spiced with odors redolent of Eastern lands.

"It is Athorama," Elfs voice murmured from empty air, "Over all this splendor Orander rules."

Blackness fell again, and, lifting, disclosed a sea-girt city, where the yellow light was tinged with a dim green glow—a white city clothed in green and scarlet, blue and purple. Vegetation wound up the towers, and serpentine trees writhed and twisted in the streets. Very slowly moved the men and women of this city—clad in flowing garments that trailed behind them eerily in the dimness. And there were vague shadows swimming to and fro...

"It is Lur," said Elf. "It is sunken Lur. And over this also is Orander a god."

Darkness fell, and lifted to disclose the amber-glowing plain on which Elak stood. Beside him was the warlock, smiling gently. He lifted a hand as Elak's blade flickered.

"Wait. You have seen these worlds which I made for Orander's pleasure, in which all moves and is ordered as he desires. Now I shall show you the king again."

The harp hummed eerily. In the ocher glow of the sky, clouds grew, shaping themselves in oddly patterned order. Slowly the vague outline of a face began to appear above them—the face of Orander, King of Cyrena. The eyes seemed to dwell on something infinitely far away. The Titan face hung in the sky, fantastically huge and distant.

"Orander," the warlock said, "here is Elak."

There was no change in the giant face, nor did the lips move; yet a voice said distinctly and coldly: "I hear."

Elak felt an icy shock go through him at the sound of that voice. It belonged to something that was no longer human. But because he knew that it was also Orander's voice, he fought back his horror and called the king's name.

"I hear," the voice said again. "I know why you have come. It is useless. Go back."

"You're putting words into the mouth of a phantom," Elak snarled, swinging round to face Elf.

"It is I, once Orander. Elf has made me a god, and he has built me worlds for my pleasure. Go back."

"You see," the warlock said, his gaze meeting Elak's frankly. "Would you rob a god of his worlds? I put no enchantment on Orander. The king asked me to grant him this boon, and with my magic I did so—made worlds over which your brother rules. Would you drag him back to Cyrena—a place from which he fled?"

Elak did not answer. A frown darkened his face. Elf went on slowly.

"Dalan was jealous of my power; that was all. He tried to lead Cyrena against me, and in self-defense I sought the Northmen's aid, for I could not call on Orander. Join me,

Elak—you can sit on Cyrena's throne, and my magic will serve you. Forget the Druid's lies!"

Doubtfully Elak lowered his rapier. "I don't want to rule," he said. "I seek no crowns. I came here to win back Cyrena from invaders, and to free my brother. But—"

"But Orander does not wish to be freed—"

"You lie!"

Dalan's voice! Elak's head jerked up. He stared at the sky—to where, beside the Titan face of Orander, hung another face, hog-fat, toad-ugly, glaring down at Elf. "Mider!" roared the Druid. "By Mider—you seek to stuff Elak's head with lies? Your spells won't aid you now—you spew of serpents!"

The warlock looked up unmoving. And the voice of Dalan thundered on from the sky.

"My magic is stronger than yours—else I'd not be here now. Aye, you seek to enlist Elak's aid, for you dare not fight him—not while he carries the Druid knife of sacrifice."

Elf's lips were twisted in a venomous snarl. But the Druid ignored him, bellowed, "Elak! There's foul enchantment on Orander. He's glamoured by the damned witchery of Elf's poison, by the spell cast on him unawares—but he can be called back to Cyrena, and he'll thank you for it. No man is made to be a god, and there'll be a fearful doom on Orander unless he's called back. Speak to him of Cyrena—of his people, Elak!"

For a second the adventurer hesitated, staring up at the Cyclopean face of the king. Then, suddenly, he lifted his rapier with a shout. He had seen something change in the god-face, and the veil of horror had lifted from the alien eyes.

"Orander!" Elak cried. "Orander—come back to Cyrena! The sea cliffs are harried by Northmen, and dragon ships

bring invaders with torch and sword. The chiefs have risen—
but they need a king, else Cyrena will fall again.

"Orander, remember your kingdom—remember the fields
of your land, green in the warm sunlight, silver under the
moon. Remember the steadings and the cattle of your
people—Sharn Forest and the Druid altars.

"The mountains and plains of Cyrena, your warhorse and
your sword, remember all these! Remember those who held
the throne before you without failing—remember the blood
and steel that make up your kingdom. Orander—come back
to Cyrena!"

The Titan face was no longer that of a god. It looked
down on Erak, the face of Orander, Cyrena's king. His
pulses surged with triumph as he heard the Druid shout,
"Shatter the jewel, Orander—shatter the demon jewel you
hold!"

Simultaneously there came a thunder and a crashing as of
riven worlds, and the ocher light vanished from the sky. The
tumult roared all about Elak, the darkness broken by flashing,
brief light-images. The ruins of sunken Lur sank down in
thunder; the huge and splendid city of Athorama crashed in
terrible destruction down the mountain, while the mitered
beasts flew screaming, beating the air with frantic pinions.
All around Elak was the death cry of a ruined universe, and it
swelled and rose to a dreadful crescendo of terror.

He saw Elf's face, twisted into a Gorgon mask of hate and
fury, rushing toward him; something like the coil of a great
serpent swept about his body. The rapier was gone, but he
remembered the crystal dagger in his belt, clawed out the
Druid blade. He drove it again and again into the cold, scaly
thing that gripped him, unseen in the darkness that had fallen.
Chill flesh seemed to shrink from beneath his attack.

Then he felt fangs closing on his throat, ripped out
desperately with the dagger. There was a single frightful

scream of deathly agony, and in a moment of blazing light Elak saw the body of Elf falling into a fathomless gulf that loomed below him. As he watched, the warlock's figure seemed to be wrenched asunder by some unseen power that waited in the abyss. And again darkness fell—and silence.

There was a low wheezing and scrambling nearby, and light flickered up dimly. Elak saw the Druid bending over a lighted lamp and realized with incredulity that he stood in the cave of the black altar. Swiftly he turned.

A man was rising to his feet—and on the stones around him lay splintered yellow shards. Orander—no longer tranced by Elf's magic, no longer under a spell. The king's eyes met Elak's.

The adventurer leaped forward, gripped his brother's arms. "Orander! Ishtar be praised!"

"Praise Mider, rather," Dalan said dryly. "And praise Orander for shattering the jewel and breaking the spell." An expression of malevolent triumph came over the ugly face. "But you've slain Elf, Elak, and for that you have my thanks. May his soul be tortured through eternity in the Nine Hells!"

From the turret of King Orander's castle Dalan watched three figures ride south weeks later. His heavy shoulders lifted in a shrug. Beside him Orander smiled a little sadly.

"He wouldn't stay, Dalan. And I'm sorry for that."

"He was wise," the Druid said. "A country should have but one hero, its king. Best let him go in peace, lest quarrels come if he had stayed."

"No. There would be no quarrels. But Zeulas—Elak, as he calls himself—is a wanderer. He will not change now, though I urged him. So he rides south again, with Lycon and Velia at his side."

The figures on horseback grew small on the plain—two who rode very close together, and one who followed at a little distance, reeling in his saddle and keeping his balance only by occasionally gripping the beast's mane. Elak and Vella talked, with soft laughter and high hearts, as they cantered onward— and behind them Lycon, in his own fashion, was happy also.

"Wine," he murmured thickly to himself. "Goatskins of it. Good wine, too! The gods are very good…"

THE END

THESE MEN HAD THE ABILITIES OF ANIMALS

The truth of the matter is that there were two Dr. Varsags. Both men were brothers, and they conducted some of the most amazing experiments involving men and animals ever recorded. Even H. G. Wells' Dr. Moreau would have been green with envy. The guinea pigs of their experiments were all human: A striking cobra was slow motion in comparison to the lethal hand-speed of premier boxer, Dexter Montrex. Try to imagine a college track star like Bart Gottlieb, whose foot speed was so fast he could cut the record for the mile in half— almost effortlessly. And finally, with the incredible abilities of a mole and super-human strength, try to imagine what someone like Professor Marvin Williams could do; especially when burrowing under the vaults of some of the biggest banks in the country. With all this as a backdrop, we're sure you'll find this amazing tale by David V. Reed to be one of the most unique pieces of science fiction you've read in a long, long time.

CAST OF CHARACTERS

DR. ARNOLD VARSAG
Not exactly a mad scientist, but he did come up with a way of transforming—more or less—a man into a mongoose!

DR. FRANZ VARSAG
He was a brilliant scientist of indelible repute, bound and determined to carry on where his scientist brother had failed.

BERT
It was a difficult position for Bert to be in, to help with a strange scientific experiment that might result in the death of a friend.

BUZZ ROGOW
From what he knew about Dr. Varsag's research, there was a real opportunity to "cash in." An opportunity he meant to take.

DEXTER MONTREX
He was a down-on-his-luck heavyweight boxer until a little bit of scientific tinkering made him invincible in the ring.

BART GOTTLIEB
It was never his intention to go out for the track team—until he discovered he could run the mile in under two minutes!

THE PROFESSOR
Try to imagine a Robin Hood-type character with the abilities of a mole, coupled with the strength of twenty men!

IRA STEINER
A fairly big-time crook who thought he could turn a scientific experiment into the biggest payday of his career.

THE UNCANNY EXPERIMENTS OF DR. VARSAG

By
DAVID V. REED

Illustrated by
Julian Krupa & Ned Hadley

ARMCHAIR FICTION
PO Box 4369, Medford, Oregon 97504

*For more information about Armchair Books and products, visit our
website at...*

www.armchairfiction.com

Or email us at...

armchairfiction@yahoo.com

FOREWORD

There were actually two Dr. Varsag tales, both of which first appeared in *Amazing Stories* in the early 1940s. The first tale, a novelette, "Dr. Varsag's Experiment," appeared in the January 1940 issue. While the sequel, appropriately named "Dr. Varsag's Second Experiment," appeared in the August, 1943 issue. It had originally been our intention to only publish the second tale since—by pulp magazine standards—it was of novel length. However, at the last minute we decided to include the first tale, too, because the two stories were so interwoven as to make them inseparable. Thus, we made the decision to turn this edition into a kind of "Dr. Varsag Saga," which we've grandly named, "The Uncanny Experiments of Dr. Varsag."

Both of the Dr. Varsag tales were originally published as by "Craig Ellis," an alias used by the authors, Lee Rogow, who wrote the first tale, and David V. Reed (real name David Levine), who penned the sequel. Craig Ellis was not one of the usual Ziff-Davis house names like Gerald Vance or E. K. Jarvis; and interestingly, author Lee Rogow's only science fiction tale, according to the Internet Speculative Fiction Database (ISFDB), was "Dr. Varsag's Experiment," which leads one to wonder why a house name would have been used for a one-time author. House names were usually used when an author had more than one story in an issue. ISFDB also lists no birth or death date for Rogow. In fact, there is virtually no info on Lee Rogow anywhere that we could find.

However, according to some sources, Lee Rogow wasn't really another author, but David V. Reed himself. The writing style of the first story is certainly similar to Reed's. Even more interesting is the fact that the central character of "Dr. Varsag's Second Experiment" is named "Buzz Rogow," who is the first person narrator of the story, which was written as though it was a "true" account. So we suspect that the whole "Lee Rogow" angle may have been something cooked up by Reed himself, possibly at the urging of *Amazing Stories* editor Ray Palmer, who might have had further mischievous plans for the Rogow/Varsag characters. We therefore find ourselves in the camp of believing that Reed was the sole author, and have credited him as such.

Even more strangely, the two tales have some very obvious discrepancies with the names of some of the main characters, which would lead to great confusion for the reader if left unchanged. In "Dr. Varsag's Experiment" the title character is named Dr. Arnold Varsag. However, in the sequel the name has magically changed to Dr. Emil Varsag. We therefore changed the doctor's name back to Arnold in the second tale. Unfortunately, one of the central characters in the sequel is named Professor William Arnold! Not wanting more confusion, we therefore more or less inverted the good professor's name to Professor Marvin Williams. Even worse, the central character and first person narrator of "Dr. Varsag's Experiment" is a dynamic fellow named Bert. Unfortunately, there is another Bert in the second tale, Bert Gottlieb, whom we have renamed Bart Gottlieb. We hope you forgive us for this tinkering, but these minor changes really make the overall presentation less confusing, without having any effect whatsoever on the stories themselves.

Greg Luce
Editor-in-Chief
Armchair Fiction

THE UNCANNY EXPERIMENTS OF DR. VARSAG

PART ONE

Dr. Varsag's Experiment

TODAY I went to the funeral of Dr. Arnold Varsag and Dexter Montrex. I watched their simple black coffins lowered into the grave and shovelfuls of earth thrown down over them. I stood there until the boxes had been completely buried, then I turned away. Yes, Dexter Montrex and Dr. Arnold Varsag are dead, and how they died makes one of the strangest stories I have ever heard.

It all started one evening when I was sitting alone in my study reading the proofs of my new book. The telephone rang and I went to answer it. It was Dr. Varsag speaking with a voice of unusual tenseness. "I want you to come over right away, Bert," he said. "It's extremely important."

I knew Varsag was excited about something, but he was usually in that state. But my proofs had to be in to the publisher within a week, and I told him so.

"Curse those proofs!" Varsag exclaimed. "This is something that will make all your inane books out of date!" His voice rose to a high pitch.

I was still reluctant to leave my work. "What's this all about?" I insisted. "You can't forever expect me to leave my work and come traipsing over to your place every time you get another one of your crazy notions."

Varsag's voice was a whisper. "All I can tell you is that it's about the Mongoose," he said. "You've got to come right over." And then he had hung up.

After that, and probably according to Varsag's expectations, it was impossible for me to continue with my own work. For weeks Varsag and Montrex had been talking about the Mongoose and all I had gleaned from their whispered conversation was that another one of Varsag's amazing experiments was under way. And this one it seemed concerned a human life—and a Mongoose. Only one thing more I knew, and that at least partially explained the reason for secrecy. The Mongoose was an extremely dangerous animal in spite of its size, and it was illegal to import them or keep them anywhere in the country because they were so destructive to bird-life. I knew that Varsag had received his specimen illegally.

I dressed hurriedly and drove over to Varsag's laboratory. His workrooms were cleverly located in a section of the city that was devoted to chemists' and physicians' laboratories, so that any late work he would be doing would not arouse any comment.

When I rang the bell the doctor himself answered it, almost immediately. His little intelligent black eyes were snapping with excitement. "I see you got here, Bert," he said evidently pleased. "Follow me, quietly."

He led me quickly into his lab and closed the door. The room was high ceilinged and very well lit. As always, it was filled with polished apparatus and tall and short and odd-shaped shining bottles full of queer liquids and potions, and as always, I had not the slightest idea as to what any of this equipment meant. The whole scene was so familiar and orderly that I forgot my mistrust.

Just then I saw the apparatus table in the center of the room, and on it a recumbent form covered by a white sheet.

Suddenly I heard a vicious animal snarl and a short burst of high-pitched humming come from a corner of the room. As I recoiled with surprise Varsag laughed indulgently, his black eyes watching me intently. "No cause for alarm," he said. "I'll show you the harmless little animal."

HE led me to a corner of the room that had been curtained off and drew away the heavy cover from an ordinary case such as he used for experimental animals. There was nothing inside that case but a little black and white guinea pig.

But what a guinea pig! Instead of the placid fat ball that never does anything but eat and sleep, the creature was fast and tricky as a fox. The animal was standing close to the front of the cage near the netting. Varsag slapped at it with a stick. Before the stick had reached halfway, the little thing was across the cage, crouched near the back, gazing at us out of its penetrating, shoe-button eyes. It was humming that high-pitched note, which had first startled me.

I looked to Varsag, but he had turned away toward a small, slanting table whose face was a maze of dials. On the largest dial a long red hand was revolving swiftly. Varsag was evidently studying it, and now he turned and faced me. "I think it's time."

"Time for what? What the hell's going on here?"

Varsag smiled briefly. "You'll find out in just about a minute," he said. "Sit down here while I get my instruments together."

He went to a sterilizer and began to remove surgical instruments from it. Then he looked at me, and was smiling again. "You'd like to ask me about it, wouldn't you?" he said.

"Damned right I would. Who or what is that lying on that table under the white sheet?"

The doctor exclaimed an angry sound as one of the heated instruments slipped from the towel and burned his finger. Without looking up, he said quietly. "The object of your curiosity is our old and mutual friend, Dexter Montrex."

For a minute I was too stunned to speak. I simply sat there with my hands clenched and my mouth tightly shut, determined not to make any outburst. And then by the time I had recovered sufficient composure to say something, it was unnecessary.

I sat there watching Varsag prepare for something...

Perhaps if you knew something of our past lives and relationships, it would be easier to understand what I felt.

We three, Montrex, Varsag and I, had gone to college together, in one of those ivy-covered New England campuses. Our friendship had come about naturally, for in those early days we had all been students in the scientific departments: neurology, bio, and zoology. In time we became inseparable, and when we graduated, we went out together to lick the world.

I did all right. Got myself a fair job in a research lab, then went out on my own as a consultant and kept going. The book I had on the presses right then was my third, and the others were almost standard texts.

Arnold Varsag had done a good deal better. He was much the most brilliant of our group, and even in his early days he had blazed with the fire of fanaticism, a restless, never-satisfied thirst for experimentation. He had gone on to medicine, specialized in several fields, and became an extremely good surgeon; even then he went on, deeper, always into science. He might have been one of the great scientists of this day if his passion for work had not taken forms too strange for most men. Recently he had passed up a chance to make a barrel of money because he was deep in some cockeyed experiments on the neural systems of small mammals.

Montrex followed the most bizarre career of all, for a scientist. After one or two bad breaks, and because he wanted to keep eating, he became a heavyweight prizefighter. Possibly to some extent this was conditioned by his love of physical activity and direct combat, which he had shown in his college football days. He was a magnificently formed man. Life rushed through that fellow.

AND now he was lying under a white sheet, while Varsag wheeled over a high table with his tools on it. Then he came over to me and sat down. "You're upset, Bert," he said, simply.

"That shouldn't be so hard to understand," I answered. "You call me away from work by mentioning that damned Mongoose that I know is around here somewhere—and then you tell me this. Why is Dexter lying there? What are you up to, Arnold?"

"Hold on now," said Varsag calmly. "There's nothing to be excited about. There isn't much time, but I think I can tell you something about this."

"It's very decent of you," I said.

"Save your sarcasm, Bert." There was a trace of bitterness and impatience woven into Varsag's voice as he continued. "Some moments ago I showed you a guinea pig. I think it must have looked more than a little odd to you. I am sure you probably have some idea of what I've done to that guinea pig."

"Only a vague one. I think you've worked out some insane scheme of cross-breeding between little animals and your infernal Mongoose."

"Cross-breeding?" There was real amusement in Varsag's laughter. "Hardly that. I made it."

"You…made it?"

"Exactly. I made that guinea pig so fast by giving him the eyes and nervous system of a Mongoose! Here…"

He rose abruptly from his chair and crossed the room. He slid open the door of one of the compartments under a laboratory table.

There were several small cages inside, and as the door slid open, the blended humming of several animals' voices filled the room. I followed Varsag and looked down. There were three Mongooses in the cages. Nasty-looking little things they were, even for a man who had had cause to become familiar with all kinds of strange rodents. They couldn't have been more than sixteen or eighteen inches long, with thin bodies, which were made to look larger because their hair was standing on end. Now they were motionless, their beady little eyes taking everything in, watching us with a curious awareness.

I felt Varsag's hand on my arm and for the moment it was as if I had been in a trance. "If we can do all that for a guinea pig," Varsag said, "think what we could do for a human being."

"Arnold!" I began.

He was walking toward the apparatus table. I followed him and grabbed him by the arm. With his free arm, Varsag reached out and pulled the white sheet away from Dexter Montrex's face. I saw Montrex lying there on the table, breathing slowly and peacefully, but imperceptibly.

"Look at him," said Varsag. "What a magnificent specimen! He sleeps beautifully anywhere."

"What are you saying?" I said fiercely.

Varsag looked at me for a moment before he said a word. "You and I have known Dexter a long time, haven't we, Bert?" he said. "We stood by rather helplessly while he fought to make a place for himself in a highly competitive world, and as much as he tried, we haven't helped him much." Varsag walked away as he continued speaking. He stood by one of the large windows and looked meditatively down into the dark street below. "Have you ever watched the way he holds his head and shoulders when he walks? He has what one calls a regal air about him. Or what other people call the look of an animal. That hasn't helped him much either."

I KNEW what Varsag meant. In spite of every physical endowment, Dexter Montrex hadn't done especially well in the ring as a prizefighter. You had to be more of a killer than he was to get by with the various plug-uglies he regularly faced. He had taken several bad beatings after doing well in his early years in the ring. His beautiful physique might have been pounded into a derelict shell after kicking around the fight clubs. All of us knew what lay at the end of that kind of road.

"What are you leading up to?"

"Imagine a creature so fast that it could dodge a snake—a snake as swift as a Cobra, which strikes so swiftly that it is literally only a blur to the human eye!" Varsag was standing there, practically talking to himself now, carried away by his own words. "Think what a nervous system such a being would have, think what marvelous speed of sight, what control and precision of muscular movement, what lightning reflexes!"

He turned and looked at me. "There is such an animal you know—the Mongoose. For some purposes, of all the living things on our planet Earth, the Mongoose has the best developed of all possible nervous systems. A human being with that equipment would be nearly invincible in personal combat. You couldn't possibly put a finger on him. He could strike a dozen blows before you realized he had started to move."*

---

* I might enlarge a bit here on what Vargas meant. In the course of subsequent days, I learned a great deal from him.

The reason that the movement of a snake, or a similarly rapid motion, is seen only as a blur by the human eye is due to the phenomenon known as retention of vision. This means that the retina of the eye preserves the image upon it for a fraction of a second. So that when we look at a moving picture, for example, we do not see individual frames of film succeeding each other, but only a continuous movement. A movement like the snake's is too fast for our slow retina to record. The retina of the Mongoose must have less retentiveness of vision than does that of the human being, since it obviously perceives the snake's motion clearly enough to dodge it. This is also partly due to the quick focusing powers of the lens in its eye, which must change focus instantaneously if it is to perceive the snake's darting motion. (There is another possibility: the Mongoose retina may have sufficient depth of focus to make unnecessary any change of focal length.)

Another important characteristic the Mongoose possesses is a lightning quick reaction time. Once decided, consciously or unconsciously, upon an action, there is no appreciable interval between the decision and its execution. In humans this reaction time is comparatively snail-paced, often taking as long as three-quarters of a second where rapid action is necessary.

The third necessary characteristic is muscular coordination, since the Mongoose must be able to change direction almost immediately, and control action with a precision to gradations involving a fraction of an inch. Indeed, a fraction of an inch is an extremely large margin, when we are concerned with the striking of a snake like the cobra, the Mongoose's traditional enemy. –Author.

I was shouting before Varsag had finished speaking. "You're not going to experiment on Montrex!"

Very quietly Varsag answered me. "You saw what I did with the guinea pig? This isn't an experiment any longer. I know what I can do, and I've shown it to Dexter. We've both made our minds up."

I stood there for a minute helpless with confusion and rage, and for half a moment I was almost tempted into violence. Standing there, watching him carefully. Varsag must have known what was going on in my mind. He smiled faintly.

"I hardly think so, Bert," he said. "Not two such old friends as we. Not when Dexter himself, as well as I, think that this is the best thing to do." He held out a hand shortly, knowing I would take it, and I did. "I am almost sorry I told you about this," he went on. "I anticipated your reactions weeks ago, that's why I kept quiet. Then, when I remembered the early direction of your work, and realizing that I would need help. I thought we could take the chance. I hope you won't make me sorry."

And so the battle that had loomed suddenly and irresistibly in my mind was quite suddenly over. There were times when it was impossible to fight Varsag. I nodded slowly in agreement...

I will not describe for you the details of that operation, for the same reason that I destroyed all notes on observations and experiments, and destroyed with my own hands Varsag's experimental animals. In spite of everything that happened, at least I knew from the beginning that Arnold Varsag was an extremely competent man, and more than that—he was honest. If his studies and notes had ever gotten into other hands...

I watched and helped as well as I could that night, half-fearful, half fascinated, while Varsag grafted sections of

Mongoose eye on Montrex's eyes, and made some extremely minute changes in the optic nerve. During this time he worked from a series of very-detailed models he had constructed from dissections of Mongooses. I might add that there was some variation made in the dendrites around the nerve center of the brain. Nothing, however, could induce me to go into the matter any further.

MONTREX was convalescent for almost ten days. During that time Varsag fed him on food mixed with a brown paste. He would not tell even me what this paste consisted of, but gave me to believe it was manufactured—unbelievable as it sounds—from some of the vital organs of the Mongoose.

Such was the splendid body of our patient that he was on his feet in less than half the time it would have taken an ordinary man after the terrific beating he took on that operating table. It is a wonder to me that he survived at all.

During this period of ten days, Varsag checked over his notes again and again to be sure he had made no mistake. He made careful and detailed notes on all his observations of the patient's condition. As for me, the nervous strain of that period was almost beyond endurance. The proofs of my book lay where I had left them that night Varsag had called, and I ignored a dozen cajoling and threatening letters from my publisher.

And then Montrex was on his feet again. The operation, it appeared, was a success. Our first impressions were that a glorious man had been created, faster and more potent than any man that had ever lived. At first I never doubted that a striking contribution to humanity had been made, except when I sometimes would accidentally see one of the Varsag Mongooses slinking around in a cage, looking at everything with that horribly penetrating, furtive look. Then I shook as if with a strange fever that might have come from the Asiatic home of the damned creatures.

I will never forget the first display of Montrex's new power. It was his first day out of doors. Varsag and I were walking with him through a nearby park. We passed a little boy playing with a large brown dog. For some reason the animal suddenly growled deep in its throat and a slightly mad look came into its eyes. It flung itself at Montrex's legs! Montrex moved easily aside and the dog's rush carried it past him. It turned and came at him again, jaws slavering. Again Montrex dodged without effort.

While Varsag and I stood by, watching the queer scene intently, a burly policeman rushed up, his gun half out of its holster. "Whose dog is that?" he shouted. "It's gone mad!"

"Rubbish!" said Varsag.

The officer spun around. "Who the hell are you?"

Varsag looked coolly at the speechless officer and turned to Montrex and me. "The dog will be all right. Let's be on our way."

Someone grabbed the animal and we walked quickly off. As soon as Montrex had walked out of its range the animal quieted and stopped struggling with its captor, though continuing its hoarse growl. Montrex laughed loudly. It was one of the few times he laughed after the operation.

"We must be careful of such minor accidents," said Varsag, "or we'll be creating a sensation everywhere we go."

He solved the problem neatly, I must say. After that, whenever a dog grew angry in Montrex's presence, and they did every time he passed, Varsag would throw a small bit of meat he carried about with him. Instead of rushing Montrex, the dog would stand guarding the meat until we were out of range. In this way we avoided further difficulty.

In a few weeks, Montrex's dodging powers increased tremendously. We used to make quite a game out of trying them. He would walk unharmed through the wildest automobile traffic, scaring motorists out of their wits, crossing through the streams of whizzing cars while the drivers looked at him foolishly.

AS his health returned completely, we decided it was time for him to resume prizefighting. There was some difficulty getting him a match, but we finally contracted for him to meet a fighter named Walloping Wharton in a small local club. Wharton was good. He had knocked out many of the big names in the ring, but he was old and could be worn down after taking a few rounds of punishment; his legs would begin to fail as the fight progressed. The usual method of fighting him was to stay away from him for as long as possible and try to get him after he had tired. Wharton was clever and a deadly puncher when fresh.

By the time the night of the fight came, I didn't know whether Varsag or I was the more excited, certainly Montrex was exceedingly calm. We watched him carefully. He seemed very quiet except for his eyes, which, though they seemed to have grown smaller, looked everywhere. When the time came to enter the ring, he suddenly adopted a curious shuffling gait, and his shoulders became slightly hunched, with his head bent forward. It was a startling change from his former free stride and high-held head.

The bell rang and Montrex just walked out to meet Wharton with his hands at his sides. Wharton, obviously perplexed, threw a raking, though hesitant, left jab squarely at Montrex. Montrex moved his head slightly and the blow went harmlessly past his head. Wharton led again with his left, this time more quickly. Again Montrex dodged.

The crowd became restless, sensing a strange situation. Suddenly Wharton started to close in on Montrex with a furious barrage of fast right and left-hand blows.

Montrex did not move backwards. He merely stood still, moving his head and body slightly, almost twitching, just enough to miss the blows, until Wharton had come in too close to do anything but clinch. Not once did Montrex's hands come up from his sides.

Wharton's face twisted into a curious expression of savagery and bewilderment. He had never before struck so surely and with less effect. And still Montrex stood completely passive. In his corner Varsag and I could see the rapid darting of his eyes. Wharton came toward Montrex again, his arms well up in a close guarding position. The crowd roared for him to knock out this strange creature who could not be touched, and yet would not hit back.

But all his efforts to land a blow on Montrex's strong body were futile. The weird spectacle lasted almost to the end of the round. Not once had Montrex raised a hand in his own defense. Not once did Wharton manage to touch Montrex with a blow. With about fifteen seconds to go, I noticed Montrex's cheek twitch slightly. He stepped in quickly and Wharton went down. He was out cold.

Yet all that Montrex had done—seemingly—was to slip forward, flash down, and send a hand forward with a single light punch. One...no more.

"Fake!" The massed cry roared through the hall, furiously. Momentarily we expected violence. But Montrex seemed composed even as he was roundly jeered, climbing through the ropes and walking back to the dressing room. His face was still completely expressionless, but his eyes were in every corner of that hall.

The next morning the fight drew comment in the papers only to be condemned as a "tank show." Only one sports writer commented briefly on Montrex's amazing exhibition of his ability to avoid punishment. The consensus, what there was of it, was that the whole thing had been framed.

WE bided our time. Only the manager of the local fight club, who had booked our first fight, was certain there had been no fraud. He called at Varsag's home while I was there two days later. He sat uneasily on the edge of a chair, his eyes traveling about the room, as if he were afraid of something happening.

It didn't take long to understand what was troubling him. He had had a long talk with Walloping Wharton, it seems, and what he had heard… "Well," as he put it, "the long and short of it, Doc, is that I'd like yer fighter to show his stuff at my club again."

There was something curious, something roundabout and underhanded, in the way he proposed the whole deal. Evidently he had some plan in mind, and was hoping we wouldn't see through it. I wagged my head for Varsag to leave the room with me, and we stepped into the adjoining library.

"You know what he's up to, don't you, Arnold?" I said.

"I think so. I think it's rather a good thing."

"Fine. My reaction, exactly. I hope we're correct."

We were correct. When our fight came up, I looked carefully all about the house, and in a corner of the balcony, I saw the evidence. Montrex was fighting another has-been named Sailor Darrel, but looking around at the names in the sporting world who had managed to find their way to this little club, I knew that the word had gone out. It hadn't taken as long as we'd thought.

I sat tensely the first few rounds. The fight was almost a replica of the first one. Montrex came in with his hands loosely at his sides and weaved easily away from everything Sailor Darrel threw at him. In the fourth around Darrel began to look frightened. It was evident he had been warned of what to expect, but even the warning had not prepared him for anything like this. After throwing a series of punches, he would back away and look to his seconds in their corner, not knowing what to do.

It was just about then that Montrex came in slowly, ducked for an instant, and flicked his right hand out. The Sailor went down as if he had been hit by a steam hammer. The fight was over. A lone voice cried out, angrily, "Phony!" but no one took up the cry. More than one pair of eyes looked up at that balcony, and when Montrex left the arena, he walked up an aisle that was strangely silent.

It broke the next morning.

There had been a slow-motion moving-picture camera secreted in the balcony—and they had photographed the whole fight! Now they knew. Where they had seen one light punch strike Sailor Darrel, *the camera showed the delivery of nine lightning thrusts*—and behind those blows was the perfect timing and muscular coordination of the fastest animal on earth!

The story was a newspaper sensation. It was ballyhooed all over the United States and every foreign country. Offers for bouts poured in by the dozens. Some bright sports writer christened Montrex "The Human Cobra," and the "The Human Cobra" he remained to the American public. Varsag and Montrex and I chuckled at that. We could still laugh about it then, about the ironical way that Montrex's speed, taken from the Mongoose, the deadly enemy of the Cobra, had given him that name. We did not dare to reveal, however, how it was that Montrex acquired his speed. After all, it was against every law of society and nature.

Then something happened that stopped Varsag and me cold for a time. In Montrex's third fight, he revealed two new habits. As he moved around his helpless opponent, he began to hum in a peculiar high pitch—and his hair bristled and stood on end. The habits of the mongoose in battle!

We cropped Montrex's hair close so its bristling would not be noticed. The sports writers did notice the new habit of humming, but they put it down to the fighter's efforts to maintain body rhythm, and some of them actually compared the habit to one exhibited by Jack Dempsey, who apparently used to hum as he moved about the ring.

The habits did not give us much trouble, but the development that they were a sign of most certainly did. In six weeks Montrex had defeated seven fighters including Young Michael, Terry Burns, Foxy Gottlieb, Cannonball Martin Pollock, and some of the toughest opponents in the ring. Varsag and I lived in an increasing state of fear, apprehensive lest someone discover our secret, and we were more and more concerned with the strange developments of Montrex's habits. He was turning into a morose and sly brute. He had almost killed the last three men he had fought, paralyzing them with the incredible swiftness and mounting savagery of his attacks.

IT was with a sharp shock that I realized he was beginning to be bored with fighting in the prize ring!

Neither Varsag nor I realized the transformation in him until the night we signed the contracts for the fight with Big Bo Porter, the giant Negro champion. For the past week or more, we had become concerned with evidences of a strange fatigue that came over Montrex at night. He couldn't rise as early in the morning as he had, and he was often tired for half a day. On this night, Varsag and I and "The Human Cobra" were preparing for sleep and Montrex had just been showing us how he had learned a new way to shave himself. Using a razor blade somewhat smaller than the usual size, microscopically sharp, and a magnifying mirror that enlarged his face many times, he cut off each whisker individually, moving his hand so quickly that it could not be followed, and still finishing his shave in half the time it took an average man shaving the regular way.

But when he put down the razor he seemed unusually morose and nervous. The recently ever-present twitch returned in his cheek. I attempted to lighten the tension by jocularity. "Well, Dexter," I said, "if everything else fails you can always be a barber."

Montrex was not listening. He put down his razor and his face dropped its lively expression, resuming that quiet, yet furiously nervous look. He began to pace about the room, turning quickly, shoulders slightly hunched. I realized forcibly that Montrex was looking and acting more like an animal every day. That quiet expression, with its nervous searching glance, was like that of an animal in a cage! Montrex was getting restless. I feared we could no longer hold him in check. I looked at Varsag and caught his glance. Was Montrex's fatigue a psychological one?

Later, I spoke to Varsag and resolved to stay awake that night and stand a sort of guard.

How futile a gesture! I could not have kept Montrex in that room unless I chained him. At about two in the morning I began to doze slightly.

A slight click roused me instantly, in time to see Montrex, fully dressed, going out the door! He had gotten out of bed and dressed without making the slightest sound. Only the clicking of the door-latch had given him away.

I ran to follow and realized I was not dressed. Quickly I shook Varsag awake and we pulled on some clothes. By the time we were ready to pick up his trail, it was impossible to trace him. We returned to the apartment.

Back in the room I turned suddenly to Varsag and said, "Montrex is becoming an animal." My voice was challenging. Varsag nodded. His face looked misshapen. His eyes were hard and black as coal.

"Our glorious man," he said bitterly. "Our gift to himself and to humanity!"

It relieved me a little to see that Varsag realized the menace of Montrex in his present form. "We must find a way to change him back," I said.

"Change him back!" Varsag almost leaped at me. A fanatical fire burned from his eyes. "Destroy the experiment?"

I looked directly at him. He saw my resolution and for once, he was on the defensive. "What good would changing him back do?" he said. "This may be only a temporary development, and Dexter would never submit to another operation now. I'm not sure it can be performed. Bert, you're not being reasonable."

"We must change him back," I said. "Dexter is our friend."

"If he is our friend, why destroy him?" Varsag cried. "I am the only man in the world who could have performed this operation and I am the only man in the world who can undo it!" He held himself erect, the lamp making grotesque light and shade patterns of his features, and his eyes shone. "I'll see this experiment through or die," he said. "And you'll see it through or Dexter dies! I swear it!"

I knew he meant it. There was nothing I could do but hope—hope that events would convince Varsag I was right. I had to stay. These men, the strange human-being-animal and the doctor who had made him, were my two best friends.

Montrex came in about dawn. He came in noiselessly. Apparently he had already learned how to open the door without clicking the latch. Varsag and I pretended to be asleep, but we watched him covertly. Fatigue lay heavily on him. His eyes were half-closed; his graceful body sagged. Sleep came quickly to him.

THE next evening we were ready to follow Montrex after he got up and left, and sure enough, shortly past midnight he slipped out again.

We followed him in Varsag's car at a distance of about two hundred yards. At that distance the sensitivity of his vision did not seem to be so effective. He walked rapidly for about ten blocks, until he came to the great Bronx Zoological Gardens, and walked without hesitation toward the zoo—and then he disappeared into what appeared to be the reptile house!

"Arnold!" I said, fiercely, "do you know where he's going?"

Varsag nodded grimly. We got out of the car and followed Montrex. We did not know then how he had affected an entrance through the iron fence that surrounded the snake house. I learned later he had stolen a key from the guard during the day. Such an act would be extraordinarily simple for a man of his speed and precision of movement.

There was an almost full moon that evening. It shone through the huge plate windows of the snake house and illumined the scene slightly.

As we looked on, Montrex appeared, *and entered the cage of a solitary cobra,* a huge creature of the breed named *Sadu.* He had stripped to the waist and thrown his clothes carelessly on the limbs of a felled tree lying in the glass house.

The reptile was awake. As Montrex came into the cage it lifted its head, with the great hood spreading out behind it. The moonlight gleamed on scaly sides as the snake coiled swiftly. In the quiet we could hear Montrex's peculiar high-pitched humming as he moved quickly back and forth in front of the swaying head of the reptile. He was only a foot away from its head…

There was a blur as the cobra struck! Montrex must have eluded the lancing movement, for he resumed his weaving

before the snake's head. The whole movement and recoil had been too swift for us to follow. The flat head whipped forward again, and again Montrex danced aside precisely the right distance.

Sadu struck again and again. Each time Montrex was untouched, coming back to the duel with his expression unchanged. It was impossible to follow the action. All we knew was that when the snake returned to position after striking, there was Montrex, elusive, imperturbable, tantalizing.

A cloud passed from the moon and we got a glimpse of Montrex's face. It was flatly immobile, but we knew that under the shadow of the brows the beady mongoose eyes were completely alive. His tongue lolled slightly out of his half-open mouth.

The bizarre combat continued. Although it took place without a sound save for Montrex's humming and a slithering noise from the coils of the snake, the whole zoo somehow sensed a fight was in progress, and mysteriously, the howls of the giant cats and chattering of the monkeys began to be heard. A vast rustling filled the snake house as every reptile in it came alive. It seemed as if the life of an entire jungle were ringed about the combatants in the tiny cell.

The battle in the patch of moonlight was nearing its end. The giant *Sadu* seemed to be tiring. Its hood dropped slightly and it relaxed its coil for a moment. The moment was enough. When we could make out the action again the snake was away in a corner where Montrex seemed to have kicked it. It was still alive, though apparently exhausted.

I was suddenly aware of Varsag's hand tightly clutched around my arm, his fingers digging fiercely into my flesh.

Montrex left the cage quickly and disappeared. The noises of the animals in the zoo subsided almost instantly. Varsag and I found the car and sped home, in order to be in bed when Montrex returned.

For a time neither of us said anything. At length as we covered the few blocks to the apartment Varsag said, "You know, Bert, Dexter Montrex is still human."

"You can still say that after tonight?"

"If he were completely animal," Varsag said, in a voice that was utterly calm, "he would have killed and eaten that cobra."

"What little human is left in him," I said, "is quickly disappearing. In a month... We've got to stop—"

"Bert!" Varsag said sharply. "We've been over this before. Understand me, now. I'm seeing it through no matter what happens..."

AND so matters continued as the time of the fight approached. We spent most of our waking hours devising ways to keep Montrex away from the snake house. Partly by tiring him as much as we could in the daytime so he would not prowl at night, partly by giving him a doped drink before he went to bed whenever we had the opportunity, we managed to avoid further visits to the zoo. On one occasion, however, nothing we did was of any avail, and we were forced to creep out into the night and once more watch Montrex go through his amazing contest with *Sadu,* the giant cobra. Again he tired it completely, but did not kill it, ending the fight by kicking it into a corner.

We trained Montrex strictly for this fight, although there was no more need of it than there was for any of the other battles. Even the power and strength of Big Bo Porter would be useless against Montrex. We only went through the routine so that he would be too tired at night to indulge his monstrous passion for those bouts with *Sadu.*

On the evening of the battle with Big Bo Porter it was of course impossible to dope Montrex or tire him out, since he had to fight a battle for the heavyweight championship of the world.

But as night drew on he became more and more restless. It was only by watching him continually and exercising the greatest of encouragement that we could get him into the stadium, dress him in his fighting trunks, and put the protective bandages on his hands. And then he stopped speaking to us. He continued pacing about the dressing room.

Upstairs a noisy crowd waited for the fight it had paid from fifteen to fifty dollars to see, thousands of people who had made "The Human Cobra" a ten-to-one favorite in the betting to win the heavyweight championship of the world. A great shouting warned that the last preliminary was over and that the championship fight was next on the program.

Varsag and I observed Montrex closely. His face was absolutely impassive.

A boy stuck his head in the door and called. "Ready!"

Varsag and I each moved to grasp one of Montrex's arms, but he evaded us easily and stepped out the door. We followed him down the aisle of the huge boxing arena. As Montrex appeared, the crowd cheered deafeningly. "Come on, Cobra!" someone screamed.

Montrex did not respond with any sign, but walked quickly up to the ring and stepped through the ropes. A muscle twitched violently in his cheek. He did not utter a word during the referee's instructions.

Big Bo Porter flexed his long, lithe arms, grinning nervously. His white teeth shone. He was a superb creature. I knew that probably he could outfight any human being in the world with his fists, but he should never have been in the same ring with Dexter Montrex. The men separated and went back to their corners. Montrex's eyes darted wildly about.

THE bell rang, and suddenly Montrex had leaped out from the corner and darted at Porter. With an overwhelming fury he lashed at the Negro, catching him squarely on the back of the neck. It looked as he had struck the champion three or four times. In reality he must have hit him twenty or thirty crushing blows at the base of the skull.

It was the back of the head attack of the Mongoose!

Porter slumped suddenly. When he hit the canvas, his head was twisted at a peculiar angle. I saw Montrex bare his teeth and look at the fallen man.

The crowd was strangely silent. The referee never began his count. He just stood there with a hand upraised, but that hand didn't come down. He could have counted to a million. Porter was dead.

In that vast and awesome silence, just as the first groan of the mob was beginning, a groan that would burst into the horrible cries of thousands, Montrex suddenly leaped from the ring. With fantastic speed he was down the aisle and out of the arena before anyone could have realized what he was doing, or raised a hand to stop him.

He had shouted only one word, just before he leaped from the ring…

"Sadu!"

And in a moment, like some huge animal awakening, the crowd was surging to life. In the midst of that overwhelming noise and confusion, with thousands streaming down to the arena, and the whole place a choked, single mass of people, we fought our way through them to the door. We knew where Montrex had gone.

It took our taxi forty minutes through heavy traffic to get to the Zoological Gardens. Through the din in the streets, and the growing shrieks of sirens, I heard Varsag, sitting beside me, cursing and moaning. The man seemed to have lost control of himself, partly from a terrible rage, more from a great feeling of frustration.

There was Montrex! Through the yellow gleam of one of the park lights, we saw him running ahead of us, straight toward the snake house.

"Dexter! Stop!" I shouted, sprinting vainly behind him. It was impossible to catch him. He left me far behind, and ran the rest of the distance to the snake house. With Varsag running grimly behind me, we kept going.

We just caught a glimpse of Montrex as he slipped through the gate, and in his hurry, he left it open. The bandages from his hands had been unwound, and they lay on the ground like white serpents.

We ran through the gate toward the snake house...and a high-pitched, frenzied humming came to us. Again the sound was picked up by a hundred confined animals. Then the faint crescent of the new moon broke through the clouds, and we saw Montrex standing inside the snake house, standing there in nothing but his short boxing trunks. A great screaming, full of wild cries, had filled the night air, yet over it all we heard him humming—watched him begin his weaving toward that great, coiled scaly body of the cobra, shining in the moonlight. Montrex—his short hair plainly on end—crouching, moving toward the glistening scales...

Suddenly the moon was shining on two scaly bodies!

Another cobra had been put into *Sadu's* cage! The two hoods ballooned. Frantically I shouted, "Dexter—there's another!" He didn't hear me. It was as if he were not of our world. The hood behind him danced, played an instant, then shot forward until its flat head had smashed into Montrex's back.

For a moment the moonlight was full on his face. His expression softened, and he spun around, accidentally facing us. A look of childish surprise came to his little eyes. Soft lines sprang up around his mouth. The humming had stopped, and now something like a sad smile flitted over his face, and it became completely placid. Then he sank down limply into the shadows. He never knew that the great cobras had hit more than once.

Then, before I could realize what was happening, Vargas, sobbing hysterically, had flung himself around the snake house and inside through the door, tearing at the heads that spit at the quiet body on the floor.

I heard him scream once, horribly. The hoods whipped about his body...

TODAY I went to the funeral of Dr. Arnold Varsag and Dexter Montrex. I have just destroyed all of our notes, and the remains of our experiment. It was a small, vicious satisfaction to kill the ratty animals, and I took it. What will happen to me now, I don't know.

I've told this story because I think it should be known. I cannot carry the whole secret within me, nor do I think it wise. I have asked the editors of this magazine to publish my story for me, because it seemed to me that within these pages, and here alone, might I find the audience for which I sought—people who might comprehend the meaning of an experiment, and not be too harsh when I tried to give a scientific justification.

For it is men like Arnold Varsag was, who make our world move. To the average person, it might have sounded fiendish. Only the men who understand such men as Varsag and, in his own way, Montrex, can sympathize with me.

Perhaps it is better that way.

PART TWO

Dr. Varsag's Second Experiment

CHAPTER ONE

I KNOW it's the Varsag story you want to hear, so I won't waste much time with introductory remarks except for a word or two about Buzz Rogow. This is really Rogow's story, you see; he even took the trouble of writing down a lot of it. It wasn't much good that way, so I got him to tell it to me. That's the way you should be getting it, if there was some way to arrange it, but I suppose this is the next best—putting it down in his own words, just as I heard it.

The story was a couple of months old by then—you remember it took the police a while to find Rogow—but listening to him, watching his blunt-fingered, oddly graceful hands moving as he spoke, elaborating or emphasizing or explaining things for which he pretended to have no words, he brought alive that whole fantastic episode in which he figured no less than Varsag or Arnold or Steiner or Prager. Or any of the many others who were part of this strange story. He brought alive those weeks of panic, and the days at the Rockford mine when—but I am getting too far ahead of the story.

It was Rogow, then, who told me the story. Rogow, the cheerful dark-faced, slightly untidy youth who had overcome a background of somewhat illegal tendency and squalor. For a while the police followed his career with genuine interest because it looked so promising, in a professional sense. He and an older brother were arrested for running a really ingeniously gimmicked wheel in a Bayonne carnival. The suspended sentence encouraged Buzz to operate a business-like racket in a fruit and produce market, and from there he elevated himself to a partnership with a shady photographer known as the Beast. What Buzz and the Beast did remained a mystery, for just about the time the police were undertaking a survey, Buzz shipped out.

He assumed an alias, Lee Furnald, and remained a sailor for an indeterminate period, but he used the time wisely. He assembled flashy evidences of an education, a snatch of poetry from Eliot, odd facts about chemistry, a little mathematics, and by the time he returned to action as a landsman, he was beyond the police in a multitude of ways. They must have been curious about his source of income—he had always been fond of luxurious living, and he still was—but he had somehow contrived to attain a certain social standing that would have made overt investigation a very delicate matter.

For in a sense Buzz Rogow was a minor celebrity, a combination of the playboy and sportsman and indefinite entrepreneur. He had friends scattered through the various social scales. You might meet him backstage at a first night or at an ambassador's dinner, at prizefights and art galleries and Third Avenue saloons. You could read what he had said in the Broadway columns, what he had eaten on the cooking page, and the society columns sometimes mentioned him among prominent names in someone's racing or opera box.

As to his income, well, he gambled a bit, and he invested in new enterprises like shows and nightclubs, and he had a stockbroker. There might be hints, now and then, that he had never really forgotten his youthful days—though he was probably no more than twenty-six or so—and that he was not above a gentle swindle, but it was always a humorous observation. Indeed, humor was one of the keys to his success, for he was a charming conversationalist. He might speak in cultured accents replete with British idioms, or in the slang of the tout or criminal or Broadway hanger-on—or, as he customarily preferred, in careless mixtures of both. It was another indication of the way his mind worked—there was a lively curiosity and intelligence behind all this—and he could be as subtle or direct as he chose. Probably he did not so much disapprove the straight and narrow as he preferred other routes, which, apparently circuitous, were generally short cut.

That was how he came to meet Dr. Franz Varsag. After Franz Varsag's brother, Arnold, had died in the strange aftermath of his experiments with the mongoose man, Rogow somehow managed to find out about the notes Arnold Varsag had left. His own explanation was that he was first attracted by a silly story about peculiar goings-on on the campus of New York University. Perhaps this was true; it sounds possible. At any rate, suppose we let him take it from there...

THAT'S what I said—New York University. I imagine it does sound odd, my saying it began there. You don't ordinarily think of a college as being headquarters for a gang of—but perhaps I shouldn't say it. Might sue me, don't you know.

Well, I was at the Stadium that afternoon, watching Fordham give NYU the annual shellacking, and enjoying it because I had a C-note on Fordham, giving 24 points. I'd get up every time the Fordhams scored and wave my maroon feather and take a nip from Prager's gin bottle, until I noticed that there was still a lot of gin left. Prager wasn't drinking much, you see. He had gotten quieter and quieter until he was just sitting there, saying nothing. As if he had big things on his mind, which was impossible, so it bothered me.

"Explain to me," I said, "that expression on your face."

Two minutes later, he said, "What expression?"

"You look as though your father's parole had been turned down."

"Oh," he said morosely, "I was thinking that we are witnessing one of the last of the sure things. Every year we come up to this game with a few of our hot dollars riding these Fordhams and we figure to make a few on this sure thing, and it is a sure thing, but it won't be that way after this year. It's just pocket change to you, but to me it's a living, and this is the end."

It was a tremendous speech for him, and I could see that he felt deeply about it. "Why?" I asked. "Are they not on each other's schedule next year? Are them NYU's finding out about instincts like self-preservation?"

"No. Next year NYU shows up with a great team."

"A fact? They buying players, you hear?"

"No," Prager sighed. "If they were buying, we could still figure out something about the team. But they're making them."

"What does that mean?"

"I don't know, but that's what they're doing."

Well, you know about Stash Prager. He's a frustrated actor, and sometimes he acts queerer than a dollar watch. So I would have dropped the whole thing except he added. "They're making a track team, too. They got a guy that does a mile in about three minutes."

"That's not much on a bicycle."

"This guy could do it carrying the bicycle. He runs."

"What the hell are you talking about?"

"My brother told me. He's a student there."

That, more or less, is how I found out. Not right then, of course, because the conversation was interrupted by another touchdown, but later, on the way home, I brought it up again because it sounded so completely screwy I was worried about

Prager's mental health. Prager had an offer once from a psychiatric clinic—they wanted to buy his head after he was dead. He turned them down because he thought they might hire agents to consummate the deal shortly after he signed.

Well, Prager told me about his brother, who was a student in the physical education department. He'd watched a kid named Gottlieb loping around the track and it seemed to him that he was making pretty fair time though he couldn't be sure. Then one day Prager's brother happened to have a stopwatch on him when Gottlieb started around. He clocked the mile at three minutes and thirty-five seconds! He thought something must have been wrong with him or the watch, but when he spoke to Gottlieb, the kid begged young Prager to keep it quiet. The whole thing, he said, was part of an experiment by a member of the faculty named Varsag.

"Varsag?" I interrupted.

"Dr. Franz Varsag," said Stash. "You heard of him?"

I wasn't sure. "So where does it go from there?" I said.

"So no place. My brother says this Varsag is from the psychology department, and he told this kid Gottlieb that he is going to make him the greatest track star that ever lived, and after that he was going to try a few new experiments that would show the rest of the fogies in..."

I LET him babble on, don't you know. I didn't mind Stash's being stupid enough to accept such a fable, but it was really funny that he hadn't even thought of the possibilities in such a thing if ever it had been true. The end of a sure thing indeed! But the damned notion kept kicking around in my mind and I couldn't let it go. I remembered how everyone had laughed at Don Ameche when he invented the telephone.

"This kid brother of yours," I said. "Is he as smart as you?"

"Buzz," said Prager, seriously, "sometimes I think he's as smart as you. He's so smart I can hardly talk to him without my head aching."

Four days later, after having spoken to young Ed Prager and patiently waiting for a break, we saw Gottlieb run. It was after school and the track was empty. Stash, Ed, and I were out of sight. I watched that kid's long legs kick up the cinders, just chugging along so easy he didn't raise a sweat, an ordinary, skinny, worried-looking kid—and my stopwatch said three minutes, fourteen and three-tenths seconds!

"Well?" said Stash.

I didn't answer until two days later, when I showed up with two new stopwatches and caught another secret workout. There was something about the way that kid ran that sent little chills through me. I'd never seen anyone go through his motions. He would turn his head in erratic jerks as be ran, his feet touching the ground gingerly, as if the cinders were hot coals, and his lean muscles so incredibly smooth in their coordination that there was a weird grace to his slightest movement.

"Well?" said Stash.

Did I say I answered Stash that day? Well, I didn't; I couldn't. I was stunned. It didn't figure. The world record was over four minutes for a mile. Six kids like Gottlieb could put the airmail out of business. So what was the answer? I could continue with fragrant hyperbole, but I'll tell you what I did—I stuck a private dick on young Gottlieb and had him shadowed. Imagination is a splendid quality, but one mustn't allow it to take the place of action.

In three days I had sufficient data to convince me that there was a definite connection between the boy and Dr. Varsag. Then I checked on Varsag, including old newspaper clippings about his brilliant brother, who died just about two years before. I caught enough glimpses of what I suspected to make it important that I meet Dr. Varsag.

It took a little doing. A friend of mine, Dr. Linkoff, of the West End Hospital, knew some people who knew Varsag and we got him to attend a dinner party. I sat next to him through dinner, trying to lay the groundwork, but it was difficult. He was a tall, bony man with huge quantities of white hair and a white spade beard. The first time I saw his eyes I thought they were very lively and sharp and merry, but later he put on a pair of glasses and his eyes seemed to go to sleep. He sat stroking his beard and concentrating on dessert while I tried to keep a semblance of conversation alive. I hinted that I was interested in medical research and I suggested that I had respectable sums of money to give to such causes. Varsag just stroked his beard and kept destroying one raspberry sherbet after another.

I was ready to pronounce the evening a failure, but when he accepted my invitation for a lift uptown, I quickly reviewed my tactics and decided on a frontal assault. When the car stopped, I said to him, "When do you plan to enter this Gottlieb boy in a race, Dr. Varsag?"

He didn't bat an eye. "I haven't decided," he said. "Good night."

THE next morning there was a telegram from him, inviting me to his home that evening. Gratefully, I lay down and slept all day because I'd been up most of the night trying to decode his answer. In the evening I went to his home. It was a huge, old-fashioned house in the West Seventies, and I could see why he hadn't been interested in my mention of money—the place was like a movie layout in old mahogany and oriental rugs. He even owned one of those ghastly butlers—the kind that when they bring you a knife, you don't know whether it's for your steak or your throat. His name was Meadows. It should have been Quagmire.

"Well, sir," said Varsag, "there's no need for preliminaries. If you'll be good enough to indicate your plans and expectations, I'll make you a handsome cash offer."

"I beg your pardon?"

"Nonsense!" He yanked his beard mildly. "I was at the track the day you turned a stopwatch on Gottlieb. The boy told me he'd foolishly let our secret out, and I was prepared. I matched your detective with a few of my own. I know as much about you as the Bayonne police. I value the secrecy necessary for my continued experimentation at a thousand dollars. Let's not use nasty expressions like blackmail. I offer it to you as a gift. You have only to find some means of assuring me that you will keep your knowledge secret and likewise silence your friend Prager."

"Dr. Varsag," I said, "this may come as a shock to you—but I'm a long way from understanding what you're driving at."

"You're a convincing scoundrel," he said, admiringly. "So shall we honor your histrionic ability and make it fifteen hundred?"

"You're convinced my object is blackmail?"

"Completely a business transaction."

"Hah!" I laughed. "But that's exactly what it isn't—not that way. Listen, Doctor. My expenses are high; it costs me some thirty-five thousand a year to get along. That means seven hundred a week to keep going. I've spent almost two weeks on you already, plus two hundred for my detective. If I take your fifteen hundred I'm just breaking even. The blackmail business isn't fast enough for anyone to live on turnover alone—so what will I live on between you and the next customer? You wouldn't want me to go hungry?"

"No. But you might give some thought to cutting your expenses."

"Make it two thousand," I said, quietly.

He was silent then. He took off his glasses and I could see his eyes again as he looked at me; those bright, friendly, understanding eyes that now were puzzled. "You're really not here for blackmail at all," he said, nodding his head. "Not at all..." and presently he added, "Will you tell me what you want?"

"Yes," I said. "There's no future in this for me unless you trust me. I got into this originally because I was curious. At first I didn't believe it—now I don't understand it. And now, after having taken the trouble to look into this, and after being troubled enough to have put a lot of thought in it, I'm tremendously interested."

"I see. And money has no consideration in your interest?"

I smiled. "I didn't say that. Money isn't my only reason for interest, but it's the primary one. The mistake you're making is natural enough—you're a good judge of people and you've intuited the larceny in my soul, but you're wrong about the method. As a matter of fact, the last thing I would want to do would be to make your work public."

"Please go on."

"Meaning why, Doctor? Because something like this Gottlieb boy, and even my suspicions can hardly explain him, is worth a lot of money to a man who gambles. Not to any man, but to someone like me. Because I know the kind of people who stake large sums on things like games and horses. I don't bet five dollars, Doctor. If you entered this boy in a race like the Columbia Mile, for instance, that bit of information could be converted to something like fifty thousand dollars, properly handled."

"That's a lot of money," said Varsag, slowly.

"It's not all, sir. I think I could probably place twice that amount in bets that he couldn't do the mile in three and a half minutes, and I've seen him do it in considerably less. By the time people understood this boy, we could have quite a sum. Possibly a hundred times the fifteen hundred you offered. So you can see why my interests actually lie in keeping your work secret."

"You say *we*, Mr. Rogow. You offer to share your winnings?"

"Of course. And the boy too, if you say so. It's only fair."

DR. VARSAG sat thoughtfully for several minutes before he spoke again. He offered me one of his Russian cigarettes and I lit his and mine. I noticed his hands then, the fingers extraordinarily long and supple, like a violinist's, or a magician's. Presently he said, "I hadn't intended allowing the boy to take part in a public race."

"But you've changed your mind?"

"I don't know," he said, slowly. "There are things to be said for it as well as against it. You've given me something to think about, young man. You've given me a new light on this matter."

"Would you care to talk about it, Dr. Varsag? Your reasons, I mean, pro and con. I'd like to have a part in your decision."

He shook his head. "Extraordinary," he murmured. "I can't believe you're the man I had investigated. Especially after your careful maneuvering last night. I was certain you were nothing more than a cheap swindler, a fly-by-night confidence man. Yet now I can't help feeling that your interest in this transcends the money involved."

"Don't bet on it," I smiled. "I want the money, though I hardly think that part of it interests you, Doctor. What does?"

He stroked his beard thoughtfully, his keen eyes on me. "Don't you bet on it, either," he said. "I'm not a poor man, Mr. Rogow, but the sums you mention impress me. If I were to enter into a compact with you, these would be my conditions: half of all the winnings go to a fund to build a new physiology laboratory; the other half may be shared by the boy and you. The money would make it possible for him to do several things he can't afford. He wouldn't accept anything from me, but this way he would be earning it."

"All right. I surrender eight and a third per cent. But what about you? You're to be satisfied with the glory, I take it?"

"With the knowledge that I had cleared my brother's name," he said very quietly.

"Then you agree, Doctor?"

"I'll think about it. I'll let you know. Until tonight, publicity was the last thing I wanted. Now I'm not sure. It may be the one answer—the definitive, shocking proof that Arnold Varsag was right, and that he failed because of a great misfortune."

I rose with him and shook hands. "I'll wait until I hear from you, sir," I said. "Meanwhile I'll ponder some way to effect a guarantee that I'd play honest with you. Of course, that works both ways. I'd want to know a few of the details of this miracle I'd be betting on."

He nodded and escorted me to the doors. Before I left he remembered something. "By the way, young man, you might tell your friend Prager to call off the detective he's had following you all week. You've an interest in maintaining secrecy, as you said. Good night."

Can you beat it? Prager with a hired bloodhound on my tail! If it kept up, I'd be leading a procession of dicks, around every time I went into a men's room.

But the important thing was that I was on my way. The beginning of the second chapter waited only for Dr. Varsag to agree, and I was certain he would. If I had had some inkling of what was to happen later, I probably—but there's no point conjecturing, is there? What happened, happened. Two days later, Dr. Varsag called me on the phone and said he was ready to go ahead.

CHAPTER TWO

IF ANYBODY ever comes along and tells you that everything comes to him who waits, tell him to wait. Then hit him over the head with a chair. The trouble with that advice is that maybe you don't want everything that comes to him who waits—things like the double x, for instance. Which is by way of saying that I could see that my old friend and bosom companion, Stash Prager, was building himself up to knife me. It didn't seem important then, but I don't believe in taking chances.

"What's the idea hiring a hawkshaw to tail me?" I asked him.

"What's the idea I don't hear from you three, four days?" he retorted. "I find you a good thing and you bid me a fond farewell. I got to protect my interests, don't I? If you're making a buck on this deal, I'm entitled to a percentage. That figures, don't it?"

"What the hell do you think you are—my headquarters?" I said. "I got to notify you what I'm doing? If you want to be my wife, say so, and I'll tell you I ain't interested. If you want to be my friend, keep your bulbous nose clean and have patience. So far all I been doing is spending money, not making it. You want a percentage? Kick in with a fast fifty bucks. You can't expect a return without an investment?"

"Where would I get fifty bucks?"

"What'd that detective cost you?"

"Fifty."

I looked at his sour face and I laughed. "So now you're broke?" He nodded. I peeled off five twenties and gave it to him. "Go buy yourself a mirror and a gun," I said. "Think over the nasty way you're behaving, then take a look in the mirror at your ugly, suspicious face and blow your brains out."

He favored me with a feeble smile. "Thanks, Buzz," he said.

I thought that was the end of it, at the time.

Meanwhile, I was seeing Dr. Varsag and this Gottlieb kid more or less regularly, sometimes two or three days running. Did I say running? Well, if it were Gottlieb I'd meant, I'd say flying and be a good deal closer to the truth. Because I saw the boy run day after day, and the wonder of it only grew. Even after I knew what Varsag was doing with him, I wasn't sure that I understood. The total effect of additional knowledge was peculiar. You'll see what I mean.

After Varsag decided to play along with me, the first thing I advised was to stop Gottlieb from running where anyone might conceivably have a look at him. If Prager's brother had noticed what was doing, others might do the same. So after that the Doctor ran him in the country, generally out on Long Island. We'd wait till the boy's classes for the day were over, then we'd drive out in my car to a little place I had near Babylon, along the south shore, and there the boy would run along the beach for perhaps an hour or so.

Little by little Dr. Varsag told me things about his work. He showed me a picture of the boy, taken almost a year before. I said that his legs looked strangely thin and weak. Varsag had nodded. "Yes," he said, glancing down the beach to see if Gottlieb was in sight again. "He had infantile paralysis as a child and he never quite recovered. That was my primary interest in this work. Or perhaps I should say that was my point of departure from what my brother had done."

It wasn't easy to believe, watching the boy run. But then, it wasn't easy to believe that you were seeing any human being running at that boy's speed. It was dead winter then, and sometimes the beach would be covered with snow. Varsag and I would stand huddled together behind a clump of bushes, stamping our feet and moving about to keep from freezing in those vicious blasts of icy, moisture-laden winds, and with us would be the kid. Varsag would give him the sign and he would slip out of the huge fur coat he wore, and he'd be standing there for an instant in a thin shirt and a pair of shorts.

HE'D dig in his cleats and then he'd be off like something shot out of a cannon. Once I turned away to blow my nose just as he got ready, and when I turned back there was nothing but a long, straight stretch of cleat tracks, and far, far off, almost out of sight, the kid was tearing down the beach. He'd run like that for an hour or so, sometimes going down for miles and then turning back, so that we'd have no idea of how much ground he'd covered, and other times, when I asked for it, he'd go about half a mile each way and keep turning back, so that we could see him. Those times he would come by, if he felt like an extra sprint, so fast he was hardly more than a blur.

Most of the time there was no clock on him. Dr. Varsag didn't like the idea of timing him all the time, as if he were a prize horse, and the kid didn't seem to like discussing the time he'd made. In fact, the whole thing was conducted almost casually, and Varsag seemed to get what he wanted from just talking to the boy. After a couple of weeks I found out why.

It came about one day when Bart—that was the kid's name—said he wanted to run on hard soil that afternoon. "I feel like really letting go today, sir," he told Varsag. "I can't make my best time on the beach. The sand gives too much and the surface isn't uniform."

"I thought you preferred sand," said Varsag.

The kid reacted oddly to that, I thought. He looked at me quickly, then he mumbled, "Yes, sir, as a rule. But not today. I haven't been doing enough real running. I couldn't sleep well last night. My legs developed a cramp. I think I'd like a hard surface today."

That interested me. I mean, not only the conversation, which was innocent enough except for something that seemed to lie in the inflections of their voices, but the fact that it led to a chance to time the boy. So I took them to a backstretch of country where there was a dirt road, now hard with frost, and fairly straight for some two miles. But I made a mental check on a giant old oak, and when I'd measured a mile from it on my speedometer, I stopped. I parked off the road and we got out.

It was a beautiful winter day, now passing into late afternoon. There was a tang in the air, and the sun was warm and bright and the sky cloudless and bland. The kind of day when people get to say that winter is really their favorite season, which is nonsense, but you know what I mean. Dr. Varsag and I were in good spirits, so I couldn't understand why Bart seemed so ill at ease.

He threw me his coat, and when he kneeled I could see his long, loose leg muscles twitching. But then he stood up again, his feet sort of pawing the stiff earth, and his lanky frame full of nervous motions. He turned his good-looking young face toward Varsag, the slight breeze riffling through his close-cropped blonde hair, and the sunlight on his face that seemed so troubled, and he was about to say something when he looked at me and changed his mind. Then, from a standing position, like the old-fashioned running stance, he whipped his legs like pistons and shot down the road.

I clicked in my stopwatch and followed him with my eyes. The Doctor was standing beside me. "You've noticed it, haven't you, Buzz?" he asked me, quietly.

"Sure," I said. "I don't know what it is, but I've certainly noticed it."

"Why haven't you asked me?"

"I don't like to ask. Part of our agreement entailed your telling me what this thing was about. You know I'm about ready to try entering Bart in the Southern Conference Mile. If there's anything I ought to know, I've confidence that I'll be told in time."

"The Southern Conference Mile," Varsag repeated. "That's an important event, isn't it?"

"Just about the most important outdoor track event of the winter season, Doctor. It ranks with the Princeton Invitation Mile and the K of C games. There's nothing like it until the IC4A games later on."

"I'm afraid I can't let Bart run in anything like that, Buzz."

I didn't say anything for a moment. My hand, holding the stopwatch, contracted so fiercely that I squeezed the stem to a halt. I lost sight of Bart then, when I turned to Varsag. "Why?" I said.

"It's too big an event. It's too important."

"We aren't playing for marbles," I said. "We can't afford to let Bart run in any but the biggest events if we're to make a killing."

VARSAG looked out over the fields, then at me. "I'm afraid," he said. "I don't know what will happen to him. I've been hoping all along that these signs meant nothing, that they would pass. Now I don't know anymore. I'm beginning to wonder if my experiment has succeeded, after all."

I shrugged. "I don't get it," I said. "The riddle's too much for me, Doctor. I pipped off several sentences ago."

In the silence I looked down the road and saw Bart's slender form approaching the great oak on his return run. I barely had time to press the stopwatch in. For a moment he was lost around a slight bend of the road and then I saw him again. On he came, running with a curiously erect carriage, his torso stiff, and his legs seeming to touch the ground with an almost awkward delicacy. And yet—all right, so I'm daft—it was with that strange, effortless grace. But more than ever, he kept twisting his head about erratically, as if some invisible fear pursued.

When he flashed by, I clicked in my stopwatch. I looked at the figures and I felt crazy and a little sick. One minute, fifty-three seconds for the mile! I didn't show it to Varsag and I didn't say anything because I didn't trust my voice. A few minutes later the kid came back. Varsag helped him into his coat. "You ran well today, Bart," he said. "Under two minutes for the mile, I'd estimate. Do you feel better?"

The boy didn't answer; he buried his head in his coat and looked out at the road as we drove back to the city, his eyes following every moving object intently. I dropped the boy at his dorm at school and when I started downtown, Varsag said, "I'd like to spend an hour or so with you now, Buzz, if you have the time."

If I had the time. I'd had nothing but weeks of it, waiting. I was ready to try a sample milking from the golden calf. I'd talked the kid up here and there, trying to sound a little potty on the subject, the way people do about their protégés, and I had elicited enough tired smiles from my friends to indicate that it was time to begin converting those smiles to cash.

When we reached Varsag's place, he took me upstairs. He had a private laboratory there, and it was the first time he'd asked me up. I went in, feeling cold and gloomy in that strange place, with the graying twilight coming in through large glass skylights I looked around at the endless rows of machines and retorts and tubes and the kind of paraphernalia you see in movies where Boris Karloff brings a stiff back from the cemetery and gives it a shot of glamorous electricity.

Silently, Varsag led me to a corner of the lab where he had a desk and a couple of chairs. He asked me to sit down but I said I wanted to stand. He opened a closet and took out a very large, thin volume and laid it on the desk. He opened it and I saw it was filled with newspaper clippings about his brother, Arnold. I'd seen most of them, as I said.

Varsag quietly thumbed through the pages, the flapping of the paper the only sound in the lab. Momentarily his face grew bitter as he looked at the pages, but it passed. He didn't have the kind of face that could stay bitter long. He leaned against the side of his desk and laid a hand flat down on the book, and when he took off his glasses I could see that his eyes were shining, but from what I didn't know.

"I think you know most of these clippings," he said. "Together they form an engrossing, morbid story of a man who dared strange experiments that ended in disaster. They are a recital of the events in the last days of Arnold Varsag, but they are not the story of Arnold Varsag..."

I KNEW what he called the recital of events. It was the climax of a mystery that read like a crime thriller, and though it had never been completely solved, enough facts or near-facts had been found to supply a fertile field for macabre imaginations. The story was that Arnold Varsag had given his best friend the reflexes of an animal—a mongoose, it was later said, and to test the transfer of that animal's speed and dodging powers, the mongoose-man had become a prize-fighter. He became unconquerable in the ring, and on the night of the championship fight he had killed the champion in the ring. Later that night both he and the brilliant Dr. Varsag had been found dead in the cobra's cage of the Bronx Zoo. There were investigations, naturally, none of them of much use, but it was a field day for a while. They called the experiments a crime against the laws of nature and man. They said Varsag's work was a perversion of science, the meddling of a madman. The stigma that was still associated with those mysterious events explained why Franz Varsag had assumed I was prepared to force him to buy my silence. All this passed swiftly through my mind in the pause that followed Varsag's statement, and which evidently waited for some rejoinder from me.

Still I said nothing, and after a few moments more, Dr. Varsag said, "My brother willed me this house. I came here from California to settle his estate and leave again. I stayed on because I found a hidden closet where Arnold had secreted the notes that were the fruits of years of work. From them, and from otherwise enigmatic scrawls in his diary, I pieced together enough to make me determine to stay here in what had been his laboratory and carry on his work. To that end I accepted an appointment from the university. But perhaps I ought to show you what is in the adjoining room..."

As we entered the adjoining room, the first thing that hit me was the heavy and not unpleasant mingling of animal odors. The room, which took up the rest of the upper story, was filled with numerous cages of various sizes, and it was illumined by batteries of overhanging lamps, which Varsag later told me were violet ray lamps, designed to compensate his menagerie for lack of sunlight. For it was a menagerie, no mistake about it. There were animals ranging from the common rabbit to three full-grown kangaroos, from toads to some two dozen assorted monkeys. I walked beside the Doctor and gazed in confusion at roosters and ring-tailed monkeys, at newts and ostriches, at jackrabbits and fuzzy sloths. Beside the odors, the enormous room filled with such a cheerful variety of noises and cries that I wondered that I had not heard them even through the evidently soundproofed walls.

The Doctor let me wander about—I told him I was looking for Prager—while he threw handfuls of food to some of the animals, and when at last I completed the circle to him, I found that both he and I were smiling. There was something about that noisy place, so full of life and sound and smell that was funny and cheerful. Maybe you've felt that peculiar warmth and good humor when you've visited a pet shop.

"It's nice here," I said.

Dr. Varsag lifted himself up on a crate, where he sat with his legs dangling. He nodded and tossed me a peanut, and for some moments we sat there quietly, shelling peanuts. "My brother," said Varsag, "was keenly interested in the lower forms. Years of keeping a house full of pets led him to some conclusions that may strike you as obvious. We all know that many animals are superior to humans in various ways.

"The sense of smell, for instance, has undergone slow atrophy among us humans. Our sight is far inferior to that, say, of the vulture. Our hearing cannot compare with a dog's. And so forth and so forth. As I say, this is nothing new to you. But what would you say to a scientist who felt that the human animal could be equipped with many of the superior abilities of these lower forms? That there was a way to *transfer* some of these abilities to humans? That the owl's capacity for low threshold sight, or the bloodhound's magnificent olfactory equipment might be given to a man?"

"Or the reflexes of the mongoose?" I ventured.

"Yes. Why not?"

"Then it was true?"

"Yes, it was true. My brother developed a method that was a compound of extremely skillful surgery and diet and training, and by his method he was able to affect a transfer of coordinated visual and muscular reflexes from a mongoose to a man. With luck he might have been hailed as a genius. Instead, with the misfortune that hounds pioneers, and with results no one could have foreseen, he was called a witch doctor."

HE BRUSHED a few fragments of peanut shells from his impressive beard and he sighed. "What wrecked him was actually a greater success than he had expected. He transferred not only the reflexes of the mongoose but other innate characteristics. His mongoose man developed a highly overwrought nervous system, a tension that brought out a killer's streak, until finally..." and here Varsag's voice grew soft and almost wondering, "finally, he grew weary of inadequate combat, bored with the absence of danger."

He looked at me a moment before continuing. "The mongoose man began stealing away to the zoo at night. There, in darkness and quiet, he would enter the cage of the king cobra, hereditary foe of the mongoose, and he would duel the cobra, dodging its thrusts, content with the play alone, until weary and happy he would return home in the morning. That was what happened to him the night he killed the champion. Distraught and unstrung, he went to the zoo that night, but he didn't see that a new cobra had been put into the cage with his old enemy.

"The coroner said that he had been struck from behind several times. As for Arnold, we know only that he followed this mongoose man to the zoo. Perhaps Arnold tried to save him. Perhaps he was temporarily driven insane by the sight and leaped into the cage to die beside his best friend. I know from his diary that he was very moody towards the end. He had begun to realize that he had succeeded too well, and he saw the enormous consequences that loomed."

Presently I said, "And you've carried on his work, Dr. Varsag?"

"I've gone ahead, yes. I've experimented with animals for more than a year. A few months ago I took young Gottlieb into my confidence. He was, and still is, my laboratory assistant at the university. He is a pre-medical student, quite a brilliant boy. He volunteered to be the human subject towards which my work inevitably led."

He tossed me another handful of peanuts and smiled wryly. "Don't think I'm a monster, Buzz," he said. "I would gladly be my own subject if it were possible. I was certain there was no longer any danger in the kind of experiment my brother conducted. I had long before found where he erred, perhaps because I was always his superior in surgery, if not in brilliant theorizing and imagination. But to eliminate any possible element of danger, I chose an innocent animal for my experiment, quite the most innocent animal I know. And I gratefully accepted Bart's offer."

I let my breath out slowly. "What animal, Doctor?"

"The ostrich."

"Ostrich?" I said.

"You wonder why?"

"No more than I would at any other animal. But why an ostrich?"

"Because there were several considerations, and the ostrich fulfilled them all. First, I wanted to try the transfer of a harmless ability. Second, in case there was any doubt as to my success, I wanted a harmless animal, so that no dangerous characteristics might be transferred. Third, I wanted, if possible, to transfer an ability that might be of value to a human being. The ostrich and its great speed afoot answered every specification.

"I considered other animals that used mainly two legs for locomotion, animals like kangaroos and rabbits and monkeys, but none ran so much like a man as the ostrich. The ostrich is a relatively gentle animal, with no predatory habits, shy to extremes, and certainly its fleetness was a valuable ability. Few animals match its phenomenal..."

AS VARSAG continued speaking, through my mind flashed remembered images of Bart running. The airy step, the gingerly touched foot, the quick, sharp turns of his head—how essentially birdlike they were! That was what had seemed so disturbingly strange to me the very first I'd seen him running! And this afternoon, his exaggerated stiffness, and the rest of it—had it possibly come to such absurd lengths? Thinking about it I couldn't help laughing. Varsag stopped speaking.

"I'm sorry, Doctor. It's just that I'm beginning to understand what you meant when you wondered if your experiment had succeeded."

"It amuses you?"

"Yes," I confessed. I looked down the rows of cages to where the several ostriches stood with craning necks, solemnly turning to examine their neighbors over and over, dismayed by the constant noise, their dark and mournful eyes popping out of their little heads. I laughed again.

Varsag said, "The failure of my experiment wouldn't be funny."

"But you *haven't* failed," I objected. "I wouldn't laugh at that; I'm really laughing more from relief than anything else. You've succeeded to a point where I can't trust my eyes. Bart ran the mile in one minute and fifty-three seconds today!"

"You just don't understand," Varsag began. "What good is—"

"But I do understand. You think Bart's adopting added characteristics of the ostrich. He likes to run fast. He likes the feel of sand underfoot. He's acting quiet and shy. It's a good case—but how would you react if you suddenly discovered that you could run more than twice as fast than the fastest man alive? Don't you think it might sober you a good deal? Wouldn't it make you feel queer, realizing what strange new power lay in a pair of legs you'd known all your life? And who doesn't prefer sand? Go down to any beach and see how bookkeepers and shipping clerks get an urge to dash about madly the minute they feel sand between their toes. If you want to keep Bart out of the important, public-crowded races because you're afraid of his developing shyness—why, with all due respect to you as a scientist and a doctor, I disagree thoroughly. You wouldn't encourage such shyness in any otherwise normal boy, would you? Surely you'd agree that the way to cure shyness was to fight it, to force the issue until it was beaten."

I felt I had been convincing, but I couldn't be sure. For some moments Dr. Varsag sat quietly, considering what I had said, absently stroking his beard. He looked, in Prager's words, like an out of the world character, his bony, long frame folded up easily atop a crate, his hair disarranged, his eyes thoughtful, and on all sides of him the cages of chattering, singing, yowling animals, and peanut shells over his tweed trousers. He munched his last peanut.

"Maybe you're right," he said, adding, "especially because I've a safeguard, in case there is any mischief. A simple operation would undo everything I've laboriously built up with Bart. I suppose you might liken it to a complicated electrical circuit—if you merely changed one connection or loosened one wire, the whole circuit would be undone..."

"So that's that," I said. "Have one of my peanuts."

"Phooey," said the Doctor. "They'll ruin my appetite. I'd like you to stay for dinner, Buzz. I want to hear what you're up to. You're so good a confidence man—now, don't object; no one but a confidence man could have persuaded me so easily—and you're so good I'm really interested in the way you operate." He smiled. "Maybe one of these days we'll try a little experiment on you. I like your mind."

"Sure," I laughed. "Maybe you could cross me with a fox."

"At that," said Varsag, "it might help the fox a good deal."

What a laugh, that conversation. I liked that business of me and the fox, don't you know, but a jackass would have been more correct under the circumstances. Not that I didn't believe what I'd said to the good Doctor, but I'd just said things that sounded right to me, thinking that if I was wrong, well, certainly Dr. Varsag would know where. But I must have underestimated my own—no, that's not quite it, either. The trouble lay in that I didn't appreciate the special kind of myopia that men like Dr. Varsag are liable to. Or maybe you'd call it tunnel vision, the inability to see very well to either side of their objective.

Why his heart was so set on going ahead with his work that he couldn't view any possible danger objectively anymore. He wanted to be convinced, to begin with, and I suppose at the beginning my point of view was that it wasn't really my cup of tea at all. Watching that boy would still occasion shivers down my spine, but what the hell! And the ostrich business was really funny; I don't care what you say.

Go watch one and imagine a human acting like that foolish bird.

It was so absurd to me that I couldn't help telling Stash Prager about it the next day. For which you can page the jackass again. But he was so damned curious, and it was on my mind, and I was feeling good at the time because I'd just laid the first small bet, so I told him the whole story. A calamitous error, to be sure, but you'd never have dreamt it, watching the way he received it, his cherubic face bewildered, his curly hair practically standing on end.

But a calamity, just the same.

CHAPTER THREE

AS I was saying, I managed to place the first bet the next day. For a G, as I recall, with Larry Swift. Swifto had quite a rep as a bad gambler, and when I primed him with talk about my boy Bart, and how he was a comer who was a cinch for the Southern, Swifto bit hard. Under cross-examination I admitted that Bart wasn't well known, that he wasn't even on his school's track team. But I stoutly maintained he would not only be on it shortly, but he would win the impending Cortlandt Park cross-country run and would then be invited to enter the Southern mile.

"Put your money where your mouth is," said Swift.

What was the wind-up? He laid me five to one that Bart, who wasn't even on the track team yet—as he checked by calling the school public relations office—wouldn't win the Cortlandt run, and five to one that he wouldn't draw an invite to the Southern, or a total of a G to my two hundred. Offhand you'd agree with him that he had something. Bart had to win, not place among the first five. And he had to be invited to enter a race that was exclusively for champions. So you'd agree, unless you'd had the uncanny experience of seeing Bart run.

Prager, who was with me, kept licking his hungry chops and saying I wasn't putting enough money down. He said I could get another ten G's in bets if I offered to take even money. Which might have been fatal, if I'd done it. You can't go around making crazy bets without stirring up investigation—not with my reputation as a shrewd article, and not when you bet heavily on a relatively unimportant event. I'd placed just enough to feel the first hook sinking in.

The kid got on the track team easy enough. He showed up two days later at the park where the cross-country team was practicing. He went over to Sterling, the coach, and he started to mumble something about wanting to run. Sterling looked at him, shrugged, and said, "This is a public park, son. Take off your pants and run."

So Bart took off his pants—he had trunks on underneath—and lost himself among some forty boys at the starting line. The coach gave them a short talk and they were off. And Varsag and I got into my car, which I'd parked some distance away like any curious onlooker, and went up ahead to about the halfway mark.

It was a good thing we did. We'd given Bart explicit instruction to stay with the pack, and to place no better than third, and to try to look at least as tired as the others. Well, the next time we saw Bart the damned fool was two hundred yards out front, with a pained expression on his face. I stood up in the car and yelled at him. He waved and shook his head mournfully, but he slowed down. He eased off gradually and he placed second.

He might have come in first if we hadn't been there at the finish line, where he could see us. He was running neck and neck with the ace of the team, a kid named Robbins, but when he spotted us, he let Robbins beat him by five yards.

At that, the coach threw his arms around Bart. "Where the hell did you learn to run like that?" he shouted. He'd seen Bart leading a good part of the way, it seemed.

Bart stuck his tongue out, trying to look fatigued, and he was breathing so hard I thought they were going to call for a pulmotor. The coach threw a blanket around him. "You're not in any too good condition, but we'll remedy that," he beamed. "Where have you been keeping yourself all season? Why didn't you show up before this? What are you, a frosh?"

And so on, but that was the beginning. They put Bart on the varsity and he ran several times a week for the next two weeks. He never allowed anyone but Robbins to beat him, and he nosed Robbins out twice. With the result that first one, then another, then all the rest of the New York papers ran little pieces about him, noticing that NYU had come up with an extremely promising junior. It was expected and unavoidable, but it had some disquieting aspects.

FIRST, it brought Prager and Swift around to watch practice. On the second afternoon I spotted Prager lurking among the nude bushes, his brother with him. I got rid of the brother, after Prager told the kid he would beat his can off if he transmitted a syllable of what he knew, but I couldn't get rid of Prager. On the fourth day, after the second piece in the papers, Swift came nosing around. That was one of the days when Bart beat Robbins. I drove Swift back downtown, and all the time he kept looking at me as if he were undecided whether to shoot himself or grab the wheel and steer us both into the East River. I was thankful I had had the foresight to warn Dr. Varsag against attending the practice sessions anymore, and I kept my mouth shut, except to remind Swift, meanwhile looking the least bit worried, that even Robbins had never placed better than second in two years in this same event.

"Rob me and kill me and throw my body to buzzards," Swift sighed, "but please don't lie to me. Where do you come off to bet that a cross-country runner will make the Southern Mile? You have something up your capacious sleeve, including tickets for a charity bazaar in my honor."

I didn't deny it, though I had warm thoughts concerning Swifto and the immediate future. Part of the plan, you see.

But Bart wasn't behaving according to plan, which was another consequence of the newspaper pieces. More and more people were showing up at practice, and they made the kid nervous. I would talk to him about his jitters some nights at Varsag's, but it hardly helped. What did help was his intelligence. He knew what was going on and he understood it thoroughly because Varsag was completely honest with him, and he was as determined as any of us that he would fight off his shyness. Sterling and the assistant coaches were crazy about him, and there was a very satisfying element in his new, local schoolboy fame as an athlete. If it weren't for his jitters, he would have been really happy.

Well, you know what happened at that Van Cortlandt run. Bart not only placed a solid first in a strong field, but Robbins outdid himself and placed as close a second as Bart allowed— about twenty yards. This Robbins was so used to beating Bart that he hung on somehow, and the rest were strung out for half a mile. But all the way I was in my car, following the race, yelling Bart's name to him now and then to slow him down. As it was, he came in just short of the record. The coach went out of his head.

The next thing was to get Bart into the Southern Conference Mile, which was less than three weeks away. The coach used to kiss Bart on sight, but the first time Bart broached the subject of running the mile, any mile, to him, Sterling started to give the kid a lecture on the dangers of letting success inflate the ego. Started, I say, because he knew better than to believe that this shy, well-mannered, intelligent kid could get cocky. The way Bart told us about it later, Sterling stopped his lecture, looked at him gravely, and said, "You really think you could run the mile, Bart?" Bart quietly said, "Yes, sir," and that was all there was to it. All except the lecture I gave him on being careful.

"No better than four and twelve, at the very outside," I said. "Stay between that and four fifteen and you're in." I was frightened because I couldn't be there, but we pulled in Prager's kid brother, gave him a stopwatch and instructions and told him where to stand, etcetera.

Bart ran the mile in four minutes, ten seconds.

That night Sterling phoned the Conference officials for an invitation for Bart. The papers said the next day that the Conference people thought he was nuts. All he had was MacMitchell, the intercollegiate champ, and he wanted to enter a second man. They said no at first, but when Sterling threatened to yank MacMitchell, they arranged for their representatives to give Bart a qualifying run.

Bart ran the mile in four minutes, eight and three-tenths seconds and posed for pictures that made a few of the wire services, and made me sick for an hour after I heard the trouble young Prager had had flagging him down. He'd run the fastest quarter mile ever done, but it was unofficial. What a stink it raised. Just short of really putting a damper on my plans.

SO WHEN they announced that Bart Gottlieb was going to run the Southern Mile, I didn't have to call Swift. He dropped in unannounced and met Prager on the way at the elevator. He pulled out an envelope, counted out a thousand and threw it down on my antique coffee table.

"Swift pays his debts," he announced. Then he counted off the rest of the money in his envelope and threw that down, too. "The sum of twenty-two hundred dollars, which sneers at your long-legged goon and backs my contention that he does not place among the first three in the Southern."

"Is that your money?" I said.

"Are you behind in your rent? Has your sister got all her own teeth? Is your uncle still in solitary? Do I ask you personal questions? I offer you genuine coin of the realm. Are you taking?"

"I hear," I said, "that there will be quite a field." I watched his face fall a little. "I hear the Conference has received acceptances from some pretty fair runners," I said. Swifto mumbled something between an oath and a groan. "I hear that in addition to MacMitchell, there will be Fenske, Venske, San Romano, Butler, Schneider, Speed Vogel, and the Rideout twins. And for the special occasion, the best in the business, Glenn Cunningham."

"You have heard too much," said Swift. "Alas and alackaday."

I pulled out a prepared wallet and rummaged about in it, coming up with a heavy chunk of moo. I counted out twenty-two hundred, which I put down on top of Swift's money, and then slowly I laid down ten crisp one thousand dollar bills in a neat fan beside the pile.

"Be of good cheer, my merry popinjay," I counseled. "Not only am I taking your absurd wager, but here is ten G's worth of green goods that my boy Bart finishes first in the Southern Conference Mile."

"First?"

"First."

"First?"

"I didn't say second."

"You said first," said Swift.

A large drop of perspiration ran down his long nose. It hung on the tip for half a minute, and when it dropped to the rug, Swift quietly sat down. He started to touch my money, then pulled his hands away. He looked at me for a full minute, then at the money, then at me. And all this time he was sweating, until the air around him was charged with clouds of vapor, like a brewery horse on a cold day. Then his chin drooped and his eyes glistened. I thought he was going to cry, but he held on. Only his voice cracked.

"You can't do this to me," he whispered hoarsely. "I'm the only support I've got. It isn't legal. It isn't fair!" He got up and began to pound my coffee table. "Dammit!" he cried. "The rich get richer and the poor get poorer! Dammit! *Dammit!*" Then, helplessly he sank back into his chair gulping in breaths of air. Presently he leaned over the table to me. "Buzz," he whispered, "let me in on it; I can be useful. You need me in this. I'm the man you need! I'm the man!"

"Why?"

"Because I can place bets for you! I can get bets where you couldn't. You're smart money in this town. You start laying paper with a few people and the market'll close tighter than a jar of olives. But me..." He laughed bitterly. "The Federal Revenue sent agents to look me up because so many guys listed me as their source of income. I got men waiting on corners to offer me partnerships in secret platinum mines. Didn't you pick me for your sure thing bets on this Gottlieb kid? I'm a natural, Buzz! They ain't born like me every minute."

"Okay," I said. "It's a deal. I can use you. Have a drink?"

HE CLOSED his eyes and let his breath come back slowly. He looked at me and at his money, and when I nodded, he counted off his twenty-two hundred and held it tightly in his fist. I took the thousand he had paid off and handed it back to him. I pointed to the bar and raised an eyebrow. "Expensive brandy, please," he murmured. He was quickly recovering his poise and jauntiness. A moment later, sipping his drink, he said, "Buzz, by this act you have acquired a bondsman and vassal for life. Your wish is my command."

"Listen," I said, "and listen closely. I expect to have maybe another fifteen thousand later this week. I can place part of it and Prager can take care of maybe five thousand, but you'll have most of the moola to play with. I'll cut you five per cent of the net for your services. Now here's the dope…"

Well done, I commended myself later. I'd gotten Swift quickly and neatly. He was damned right I needed him! But I'd also given him a handsome deal, and while I don't like to go around piling up debts of gratitude, I felt pleased. Swifto was an honest guy with incredible amounts of bad luck. The only reason he never killed himself was because he was afraid something worse would happen to him if he tried.

Within ten days he had plastered the town with my money—twenty thousand worth, at varying odds, some on Bart placing among the first two or three, some—not too much—on his placing first. Added to what Prager and I had placed, if Bart—I mean *when* Bart placed first, I'd stand to collect something over seventy-five thousand. It was a lot of money, and I wondered if I had overdone it for a first try. That was before I found out what Prager had done.

He had taken the five thousand I'd given him and gotten an average of fifteen to one that Bart would do the mile in under four minutes!

I almost went out of my head when he told me. He sat there, his mouth drooling, telling me who he had hooked and asking me over and over what his cut was going to be. He had raised the winning stakes to close to a hundred and forty-five thousand dollars! I know, I know. When you talk about that kind of money it stops having much meaning. It's like counting beans in a jar. When the paralysis passed, I stumbled across the room and picked up one of the andirons. I'd have killed him if Swift hadn't hit me over the head with a bottle.

But after that there was nothing to do but go the rest of the way. I hocked everything but my stopwatch. I mortgaged my beautiful custom Cadillac down to the chromium exhaust pipe. My country place, my apartment and all its furnishings including the silver frame on my grandfather's picture, my bank balance and everything I could borrow in a hurry—the works—I put it all down as fast as I could, wherever I could, but not too much in any one place. I didn't want anyone leaving town. And when I was through, I had more than fifty-five thousand down, with the expected take close to a quarter million. I don't know what it might have been if the odds hadn't fallen off quickly when my money kept showing. A quarter of a million. Don't even think about such things.

I saved a little. I needed money to pay the six bodyguards I got for Bart. Then I bought round trip plane tickets to Miami for Swift and Prager—he was in it, so what could I do?—and myself, and I had some money for food and aspirin. I was like crazy the week before the race. I followed Prager from one steak house to another, watching him eat. Dr. Varsag examined me twice and gave me sleeping pills. Winchell wrote: *"Friends of Buzz Rogow reported seriously worried about his health. The story is that he spent his money on an invention to grow zippers on bananas. Now he thinks people follow him."*

Only I didn't think. I knew it. Some of the people were Shylocks to whom Prager owed sums like six dollars, and who I paid off with the money I saved by not eating. Who the others were I didn't know, but they were there. You can't go around getting rid of that kind of money in a week or so without raising dust. Every other guy I met had a question in his eye. If I went anywhere I had a fleet of cabs following me. The DePuys invited me to the opera and batteries of binoculars gave me the once-over as I sat in the box, and I averaged a dozen flirtations with high-class floozies between every act.

It was bad, don't you know, but there was one bright spot. I kept telling myself that. If it was going to be one shot, at least it would pay off. Maybe later I could try again, betting that Bart could do the mile in under two minutes, so maybe the comment was all to the good. Not that it was comment, particularly. Not many people actually knew what was cooking, but the wires were up, as they say in Harlem. People knew *something* was cooking.

That was the way things stood the day we flew to Miami. Ever been in one of those big passenger planes? The door opens easily. You unlatch a lever, then you push hard against the wind, and then there's nothing but seven thousand feet of cool air between you and the ground. I knew all that. If I'd known more, I'd have opened that door and stepped out.

But I'll tell it to you the way it happened...

I DIDN'T dare see Dr. Varsag until the morning of the race. I went to the hotel where he had been staying a few days and gave him an accounting. In round figures the calculated take was two hundred and forty thousand. Take off half for Varsag's fund: one hundred and twenty thousand. Half of that to Bart left sixty thousand. Swift's five per cent plus a cut to Prager plus my expenses left me fifty thousand. I had put up fifty-five to win fifty.

"Good Lord, Buzz," said Varsag, "stop trembling."

"How?" I said.

I sat there another hour, waiting for Bart to arrive. I found a hypodermic syringe and Varsag caught the gleam in my eye. "Go ahead," he said. "It won't harm you."

"What is it?" I said.

"An experimental serum for hoof-and-mouth disease."

When Bart finally arrived, he was accompanied by coach Sterling, an assistant coach, and the bodyguards, now increased to eight. Sterling couldn't understand what Dr. Varsag was doing there, and when I was introduced to him, he screwed up his face and looked as if someone owed him an explanation. He didn't get it. Varsag listened to his complaints quietly, agreed with him, but pointed out that Bart and he, Varsag, were good friends and if Bart wanted to see him...

"But these bodyguards!" said Sterling. "Who's paying for them? The minute Bart sets foot in the street they follow him. They came down on our train, and they've managed to get official's passes for the track. They're driving Bart crazy. Isn't that so, Bart?"

Bart was busy chewing something, but he shook his head. Only he shook it seven or eight times, like you shake a mop on a window ledge. He kept turning and looking from one to the other of us out of the corner of an eye. He didn't look very nervous, but if you looked at him *you* started to shake all over. Not me; I was shaking to begin with, but he had the bodyguards twitching like mad. After Varsag got rid of Sterling and sent the bodyguards down to the lobby, we both spoke to Bart.

"You're all right, aren't you, Bart?" Varsag asked him. "I want you to tell me the truth. You understand what's worrying us."

All he got for an answer was a loud gulping sound. Bart had been standing facing a window, so I walked around to where I could see his profile. The huge wad he'd had in his mouth was gone. He'd swallowed it, I thought, but somehow, from the way he'd been chewing, I'd supposed he was chewing something unswallowable, if you get what I mean. I sat down and continued watching him, while Varsag spoke. Sometimes a wide, foolish grin crossed his face. When the Doctor finally went to the phone to order lunch, Bart crossed to another window and he actually strutted like a drum major. Or like a damned ostrich! You heard me. He had the pop eyes and the grin and the walk of an ostrich!

"Eggs for me, Doctor," said Bart, quietly, grinning. "About six hard boiled eggs. They're good for me. And toast and milk."

He seemed almost all right then, and while we had lunch I spoke to him, I told him that he'd have to be careful when he ran, that he was to make the mile in just under four minutes, and to pay strict attention to the signals of the coaching staff, who'd let him know where he stood all the way. "Stay with the pack most of the way," I said. "On the last lap put on a driving finish, not too fast. That'll do it. If you—"

I didn't finish what I was saying. The Doctor wasn't looking and he thought I didn't see. He had opened one of the eggs and was eating it, but with a swift movement he picked up one of the other eggs, and shell and all he swallowed the egg whole! It disappeared down his throat in one smooth gulp. He grinned and went on eating the other egg. I almost choked at the sight, but I said nothing. I felt if I tried to say anything I would shriek. Bart ate three of his eggs like a man, and the other three he just threw into his gullet.

And Varsag, talking on and on about his experiments, never saw a thing. At the end of the meal he remarked that he had never known Bart was so fond of eggs, and mightn't they be harmful before a race?

"I like 'em," Bart smiled. His Adam's apple jiggled when he spoke.

We drove him to the stadium and on the way, sitting beside Bart in the car, I watched him carefully. He had a bag of enormous candy drops in one of his pockets, and he would surreptitiously swallow one of them from time to time. When they were gone, his fingers seemed to have nothing to do, so he toyed with one of the buttons of his coat. I must have looked away for a moment, because the next time I looked, the button was gone and Bart was grinning.

BY THE time we reached the stadium the other two buttons had also disappeared, and, I was afraid, my sanity. I almost blurted the truth to Varsag. I couldn't stand it. But I remembered that I was in a hole that reached almost to China. A few hours wouldn't make any difference. I would tell Varsag everything immediately after the race. How was I to know that I would never see the end of that race?

I remember the way the Miami Stadium was that day. It was a beautiful day, warm and pleasant, and the air filled with good cheer. It was a Saturday afternoon, and countless thousands filled the streets leading to the stadium, and inside there were pennants and school banners and bands, and lovely women and everything that goes with a great sports spectacle. But I walked along like a drunk, braced against Prager and Swift, wondering where I'd lost Dr. Varsag, thinking of hard-boiled eggs.

There were about two dozen people I knew, and I kept shaking hands automatically, and after we were in our box I leaned against the rail and waited through the early events with eyes closed, because everywhere I looked I saw Bart. The waves of sound all around me were like insulation against my fears, and in the midst of the shouting and yelling I found peace. And then I became conscious of a growing quiet, punctuated again and again by tremendous shouts, but the intervals quieter all the time, with a hushed, suspenseful note, and I heard the announcements and knew that they were getting ready for the Southern Conference Mile.

I opened my eyes and I knew I was seeing sports history. They had the greatest gathering of milers that ever trod the cinders there, and as each star appeared, he was greeted with an ovation. Cunningham, a little older, but one of the all-time greats, the redoubtable Fenske, the good-looking Rideouts, Butler the arrogant, the dogged Venske, MacMitchell in his best year. Bart came out with MacMitchell and shared his cheers, and Archie San Romano followed, and then Speed Vogel.

Sterling was talking to MacMitchell. Then he went to Bart. I saw that Bart was holding his fists tightly closed. He was twenty yards away, but I could see how pale he was, how stiff his legs were. Every time the crowd yelled he winced. He had stopped dead for an instant when he first came out and faced the shout from the forty thousand people who ringed the cinder track, and only the succeeding shout when San Romano followed had made him move again, and then he had jumped forward as if he had been struck a stinging blow.

The starter called the entrants together and a roar of noise rolled through the stadium, followed by a thrilling silence. In that silence the runners crouched down, all except Bart, who remained standing stiffly, legs together. Sterling shouted at him; the starter spoke to him, but he stood there. The starter raised his pistol.

"On your mark...! Set...!" *Bang!* The pistol cracked sharply and the runners were off. But Bart hadn't started with them! He had jumped at the sound of the pistol, and then as the crowd came to its feet with a mighty shout, he leaped forward, a flashing streak!

In ten yards he had caught them.

Then he was past them. He was running faster than I had ever seen him run before. He was like something shot out of a catapult, his long legs striding stiffly, his arms tight against his sides. In a hundred yards he had picked up a thirty-yard lead! The crowd, electrified, responded with a single, mighty shout that was torn from the throats of forty thousand people.

For an instant Bart wavered. I could see his pitiful face. He flashed by me and I saw the terror in his eyes, his mouth crazily askew. He raised his arms and covered his face with his hands, trying to blot out the sight and sound of those frenzied thousands. Faster and faster he ran. At the hundred and fifty yard mark he was fifty yards in front. The roaring grew to thunder, louder, louder, louder…

And then it happened.

Suddenly Bart swerved from the cinder track, ran across the inside of the track and hurled himself into a jumping pit and buried his head in the soft dirt!

All I remember of what happened after that was the noise. It seemed to fill the whole world. For a few moments I continued to look at the pit, but it blurred, and my brain was filled with the noise, and I was rushing through people.

CHAPTER FOUR

WELL, that was the beginning. Yes, that's what I said, the beginning. Not of the part of this story that concerns Bart, of course, but of Williams and Steiner and the rest. There was this division between these two sequences of events, the one depending on the other, so I think of the Bart part of it as the beginning of the other, the really— Bart, you say? But of course I'll tell you about it. Just let me tell it as I see it. This is the part you wanted to hear about, isn't it? All right, then.

There comes a time in every man's life when he decides how much he can take. Some break so hard the lesson is permanent, and they don't live to remember what broke them. Like that epidemic of stockbroker's disease in the early thirties, when you couldn't walk through the Wall Street district without an iron umbrella every time the market went sour. And some men bend. Maybe it's a thing you get used to doing. You take enough and you learn to bend. Maybe that's why when a man tries to find release in drinking they say he's on a bender. It's a thought.

I'm the bending kind. I don't get drunk; drinking only makes it worse. What I do is go someplace and sit down and remember. I think of the time I had tropical fever in Peru, or the time I served thirty days for vagrancy in Missouri, or the time—I was a kid then—when I won thirty thousand dollars on the horses in Rio one afternoon and lost it in roulette that night on a gimmicked wheel. I know wheels, brother.

So that by the time Swift found me three days later in Coral Gables, I was all right. I'd taken one bus after another as long as my money held out, not caring where I was going. I wound up in Coral Gables and Swift, who had the police out checking railroads and busses and airlines, traced me there. I was sitting on an old box near the seashore when he walked over and sat down beside me.

"Hello, Buzz," he said. "How's it going?"

"Nice," I said. "Pretty nice."

He gave me a cigarette. When I finished, we went into town and he bought me some ham and eggs and I went to a barber and got a shave and then I had my suit pressed. Then we took a train back to Miami and he paid our hotel bill. Prager was gone. They were all gone. The town was quiet; it was towards the end of the tourist season. I wanted to hang around a few days. Sort of haunting the scene of disaster because I didn't want to run away. I wanted to file it with those other memories.

Two days later, at Swift's insistence, we went fifty miles up the coast and spent a few more days in a drowsy little town.

We slept late and went fishing and drank beer. And after awhile we talked, and he told me what had happened. I hadn't looked at a newspaper. He told me how Varsag had taken the kid away, no one knew where, and how the papers had gone crazy. The kid had run a hundred and fifty yards in eight seconds or thereabouts. Naturally there was talk about Varsag. Sterling had shot his mouth off, and everyone began remembering Arnold Varsag and his mongoose man. The university suspended him—he was still missing all this time— and there was clamor for an investigation, but no one knew whether New York or Florida had jurisdiction. And so on.

I wondered how it would come out, but I remembered Varsag's telling me that he could easily undo his work, so I wasn't worried about that part of it. The boy was intensely loyal to Varsag, and when he had been brought back to normal, there was no doubt that he would stick by the Doctor and disclaim everything. They'd never prove a thing. I was the only other person who knew about—but I wasn't! Prager knew. I'd told Prager that day when I found out. And that was no good.

So Swift and I went back to Miami and took the first plane to New York. The apartment was still mine until the first of the month when all the notes would fall due, so I went there. When Swift and I got into the elevator, the boy said that several of my friends, including Mr. Prager, had been living there for the past week. They'd said I told them it was all right, and the superintendant knew Prager, and was it all right?

I OPENED the door and there was Prager, without a shirt, and two more men with him in the living room. A third came out of the kitchen. He was wearing an apron and holding a frying pan.

"What the hell is this?" I said.

One of the men near Prager got up and walked right past me and closed the door, pushing Swift away. He leaned against the closed door and said, "Sit down, Buzz."

"I don't get it," I said, "and I don't like it. This is—"

The man said, "Did anybody ask you what you like? Sit down, both of you." He put a hand into his jacket and took out a large, dark blue automatic. He didn't point it at me. He let the weight of the gun pull his arm down, so that it hung loosely, the gun pointing to the floor. He said, "Make it easy on yourself, Buzz."

I walked across the room and picked up the phone. Prager cried out, "Buzz, don't!" The man who was sitting near him sat up a little and shook his head at me, his forehead creased into a frown.

I was dialing SPring-7-3100. The man who had been in the kitchen put down the frying pan and came over to me quietly and watched the first four holes I dialed. Then he wiped his hands clean on the apron, turned me around, took the phone out of my hand, and punched me in the face. I fell down to the floor. He stood over me, still holding the phone, and when I got up, he hit me again. I sat on the floor after that, leaning against a chair. I couldn't see out of one eye.

Then he dialed a number. "Ira?" he said. "Max. He just got in. No. No. Swift. Me and Harry and Frank. Prager too. Sure."

After he hung up he went back to the kitchen. I could hear him frying bacon and cracking eggs. The other two, Harry, who had been at the door with the gun, and Frank, who sat near Prager, sat down at the table again with Prager. They had been playing pinochle with Prager and they seemed very intent on the game because Prager was winning. Swift sat in a big armchair not far from me but he didn't say a word. I got up and went into the bathroom and washed the blood off my face. When I came out, Max was bringing out four dishes of bacon and eggs. They talked about horses while they ate, all except Prager. He never said anything, and he was hardly eating. His eyes kept straying to me, and they were more frightened than I had ever seen them.

They were having coffee when the doorbell rang. Harry looked through the peephole and opened the door and Big Ira Steiner came in. I'd wondered if Max was calling Ira Steiner, though I didn't know Max or Harry or Frank, but the name Ira meant something to me. Now I knew. Ira threw his tan polo coat on a chair and came over to me. "Hello, Buzz," he said, pleasantly. He looked at my face and he turned around to the others. "What'd I say?" he said, going over to the table. He had thick, loose lips that hung open most of the time, but now he wet them and kept them tight. He looked from Harry to Frank to Max through the thick lenses of his glasses that made his eyes enormous. "What'd I say?" he said.

Max said, "He tried to phone the cops."

Steiner looked at Max. Max was about twice my size, with hands like bowling balls. Steiner was big too, but his reputation was the really big thing about him; it made his size unimportant. He picked up Max's half-filled cup and threw the coffee in his face. He stood next to Max while Max took out a handkerchief and wiped himself dry. "I don't talk to hear myself talk," Steiner said. Then he came over to me.

"I'm sorry, Buzz, he said. "You all right?"

"I'm all right," I said.

"I'll tell you how it is," he said. "I got maybe twenty-five G's of what you laid around. I sent my boys around picking up after you. I got interested in what you was doing. You know I got a great admiration for you, Buzz. I think you got a head on your shoulders."

"Thanks."

HE PULLED the cellophane wrapper off a cigar. He looked at me with his huge, staring eyes and he waved the cigar gently in acknowledgement. Then he took out a pair of clippers. "Just the same," he said, "I hear you lost a lot of money. I hear you're broke." He clipped the end of his cigar. "But just the same, I think you got a good head."

"Spill it," I said. "It's a big buildup."

"I think it's worth it," he said, lighting the cigar. He stared at me. "Tell me about your friend and the animals."

I let my breath out. "I don't know what you mean," I said.

"I mean Dr. Varsag and his monkeys and ostriches and rabbits."

When I said nothing for a minute, he said, "Don't stall, Buzz. I got no time to waste. I got most of the dope from Prager a couple days ago. I got enough to know what I'm after."

Suddenly Prager jumped up. "They hit me, Buzz!" he cried. "They made me tell them! They kept hitting me until I couldn't…" He stopped speaking just as suddenly. Steiner had turned around in his chair, waiting for him to finish. When Prager silently slumped into his seat again, Steiner turned back to me.

"Don't believe that fat slob," he said mildly. "He shot his yap when he was peddling your bets around town. Making cracks that the other boys are up against a human ostrich." He waved his cigar apologetically. "I've got to investigate cracks like that, Buzz. Fifteen to one…that's a lot of money for someone to lay on under four minutes for the mile. But we didn't hit him. After what happened in Miami, we just asked him and he told us. I don't like to hit nobody, Buzz. I like for people to tell me when I ask them. Like I'm asking you."

"You said you know already," I said. "Why ask me?"

Steiner nodded. "Don't get nervous. I'll make it short. I got most of what I want, like I said. But you can help me, Buzz. I got an idea that might pay off big. Very big. Big enough to make your little scheme look like coffee and cake money. I'm not saying this against you. You got a good head. But this is big." He licked his lips. "Millions, maybe. Interested?"

"Maybe," I said. "Where does Dr. Varsag come in?"

"He's your friend. He owes you something. He might do something for you if you worked out a nice way to get him to do it.

"Is it true what Prager told me? Is it true that Varsag can fix a man so's he'll be like an animal he picks? Like his brother did with that prizefighter who wanted to kill snakes, and this kid who turned into an ostrich? Can he do that? Yes or no."

I said, "You haven't answered my question."

Steiner waited a moment, then he said, "Buzz, I'm giving you a chance to come in with me. I can get along without you. I told you I know the answer. I just want to hear it from you. I won't ask again."

I'd been thinking while we spoke. I knew he wasn't as sure as he said he was. I knew that if I corroborated Prager it would relieve him, but even if I disagreed, it wouldn't stop him, whatever he was up to. Prager had known almost as much as I did, and I knew he had spilled his guts. I could gain nothing by denying it. I could find out what he was doing by admitting it. If he needed my help, there would be time to make another decision.

I thought of the other elements too. The money, for instance, though it wasn't too important then. Or what he might do to Swift and me if refused. That he would play honestly if I was honest with him I hardly doubted; in his own way, Steiner was square. He was a big enough cutthroat and gangster to be able to afford such luxuries.

"It's true," I said.

"Okay," said Steiner, getting up. "Get your things on. We got a trip ahead of us." He had turned around, talking to his three hired hands, but he kept looking at Swift. He looked from Swift to me as if he was going to ask me something, but he saw the answer in my eyes. "You too," he said to Swift, shaking his head. "We'll need a bus before we're through," he growled.

When we got downstairs, Steiner and Harry went with me in my car, and Prager and Swift followed with Max and Frank in a huge maroon limousine. Steiner asked me where my bank was and I told him. "Let's go there first," he said. I drove uptown. Maybe I had ideas when we passed cops, but I didn't try any of them. New York is a big town, but Steiner could find me in it if he wanted to; besides, I had nothing on him.

Outside my bank Steiner handed me an envelope. "There's twenty-five thousand inside," he said. "Deposit it in your account. It's the dough I won from you. I can spare it."

"My mother told me not to take candy from strangers," I said.

"Very funny," said Steiner. "Consider this a down payment for reasons of good will. You owe a dozen guys and I don't want them coming around, or taking away this nice car and your apartment. You'll be able to send them checks this way. And don't bother me with questions."

After I made the deposit, Steiner told me to drive up to West End and Seventy-first. I parked there and Steiner went into a house on the corner. A few minutes later he came out with a very small man who wore a blue slouch hat and a fuzzy dark coat, and who carried a black bag like a doctor's. Steiner put him in the back seat with Harry.

"Buzz, this is Professor Williams," said Steiner.

The little man stretched forward a hand. It was a wiry but very delicate hand. "Charmed," he said cheerfully. "Call me Professor."

Steiner stuck a hand out of the car and waved to the car behind. It shot forward and I followed. We kept going uptown until we came to the Washington Bridge, and after we crossed it, I asked Steiner where we were going.

"To London town," the Professor called, "to make our fortunes."

That was all the answer I got. We kept riding...

WE RODE for some three hours. We crossed through a strip of the north Jersey roads and went upstate through Middletown and Monticello and then turned off the main road. We were in the lower Catskills. On this bleak March day they were cold and deserted, the towns still asleep like hibernating animals. By the time we reached Woodbourne the day had turned to slate-gray twilight, washed by intermittent rains.

We stopped in Woodbourne and Steiner went into a bar, where I saw him go into a phone booth. Then he waved the other car ahead again and we followed. We drove perhaps two more miles and turned up a dirty road. A man in a drenched raincoat was waiting for us at the turn. He got on the front right fender and flashed a light, which was answered from a large greystone house at the end of the road. We stopped at the house.

When we went in, we were greeted by a fire in a large fireplace and delicious odors of food. A Chinese cook named Jimmy stuck his head into the living room and called hello to Steiner, and Steiner introduced me to the two men who had been there with Jimmy. One he called Flipper and the other

Pittsburg. I knew Pittsburg; I'd met him around at crap games. Flipper looked enough like him to be his brother.

And now the atmosphere changed. The house was well furnished and comfortable, in a countrified way. The radio was on and we listened to the Make Believe Ballroom and Harry did a soft shoe dance on the hearth in front of the fire. Pittsburg was whistling and mixing old-fashioneds and it was very cheerful. We all sat around and relaxed. I felt relaxed too, don't you know, in spite of everything, and the drink helped. So I spoke to Swift and said I wouldn't worry if I was him and Steiner winked at us and indicated Prager, who was peeping into the kitchen. I tell you it didn't look much like a design for crime.

Sure it was crime. What else, with Steiner in it? But I didn't know more than that until half an hour after dinner. We ate big steaks and baked potatoes and salad and good coffee, and then there was some Band B, and all during dinner a lot of talk about horses and girls and what there was to do around this part of the country, as if it were understood that we were staying there for a while. Once Prager started to tell a story about how he had had a job as an actor near Woodburne, but nobody believed him and he shut up.

But after dinner Steiner waited a bit, and then asked the Professor and me into a study that adjoined the living room. I'd watched the Professor during dinner. He was a smiling, good-natured person with a sly sense of humor. He didn't seem to know the others very well, all except one or two, and mostly he spoke to Steiner, who obviously liked him and frequently repeated the jokes the Professor made. The Professor would crack one, pull on his sharp, bird-like nose, and remark, "I ought to send that in to Winchell. Or Sobel; more his style, I think." When we went into the study, he took my arm in a fraternal way.

Steiner lit a fresh cigar. I sat on the edge of a large desk, facing him and the Professor. "Buzz," said Steiner, "the reason I took you all the way up here is your friend, Dr. Varsag. I followed his tracks. He and the runner kid are up the road about a quarter mile. They been holed up there since the Miami fizz. It works out nice for me. If Varsag was in the city, we might have to bring him to a place like this. But this is nice. I rented this place last week to be near him."

He blinked at me through his thick lenses. "That's number one. The Professor here is number two. You know him." When I shook my head Steiner said, simply, "William the Finger."

The Professor nodded, smiling at my startled exclamation. "William the Educated Finger," he amended. "Also known as The Finger, The Scientific Finger, Williams the Finger, Professor Wade Williams, Professor Lightfingers and many, many others. I prefer Professor."

WELL, I didn't say anything. What was there to say? Of course, I knew him. I recalled what I'd thought when I first saw him carrying his little black bag and it made me smile. I had the honor to be in the same room with an internationally famous crook. I say crook because he was exactly what that rather old-fashioned word conjures up—the old-fashioned crook, the kind they don't breed anymore, the masters and real craftsmen, the artists. Sometimes men like the Professor light only the relatively obscure pages of police blotters and jail rosters; sometimes an author comes along and brings, say, a Jimmy Valentine to the attention of the world. It wasn't necessary in this case.

That was Professor Lightfingers. A few years ago George Raft played a lead in a movie that was built around one of the chapters in the Professor's life. There was an item in the Times that Simon and Schuster had persuaded him to write his autobiography for them. Every time a big safe surrendered to cunning, the police sent around a messenger to pick up the Professor's alibi. Before the Safe and Loft Squad did anything on these big cases, it was said, a special Alibi Squad first went over the Professor's alibi. Two years before he had been on the cover of *Time;* that was on the occasion of his fourth and final announcement of his retirement, when he was tendered a testimonial dinner at the Waldorf by the Detective's Mutual Aid and Benevolent Association.

I bowed from the waist. "I beg your pardon," I said. "I should have recognized you, Professor."

"Quite all right," he acknowledged. "My retirement, no doubt." He rippled his fingers. "I feel like a new born babe, fresh in the world. I have dear Ira to thank for making life so promising once more."

"Nice," said Steiner. "So that's number two." He opened the door and called out, "Pittsburg! Bring me a mouse!" He waited until Pittsburg brought him a covered, medium-sized cage, then he closed the door and put the cage down on the desk. "This is number three," he said, taking the cover off the cage.

I looked at the scratching, blinking animal. It was the size of a rabbit, dark brownish-black with peculiar, large claws.

"That's not a mouse," I said.

The Professor nodded. "A mole," he said, softly. "An English mole. Think of it. Ira says you are very intelligent. Think!"

I looked at the creature, then at Steiner, then at the Professor. I backed away from them. I thought I would choke if I didn't catch my breath. I kept shaking my head, and I heard my voice saying, "No, no, no," over and over. The sweat ran down my face.

"For the man who operates in darkness," the Professor said, very softly, "who breaks in where he is not wanted, who digs in to avoid pursuit. Think, my boy. Think of what it would mean to combine the talents of the English mole and The Scientific Finger…"

I sank down in a chair, unable to take my eyes off the fat, half-blind little animal in the cage, watching it scratch away at the bottom of its cage. The sound of its claws was the only sound in the room for a long minute, and then I became conscious of the radio and the voices in the other room. I shook my head.

"You mean no?" said Steiner.

"No."

"Jerk," said Steiner, taking a long pull on his cigar. He had a disgusted look on his face. "Why can't you do things nice?" he asked. "Here I was feeling good, having two people like you and the Professor in this with me. What do you think I'll do—give you and Swift a bus ticket home and call it off? You want me to hurt Varsag's kid, maybe? You want me to make trouble? I don't like trouble."

"The kid?" I said. "No. You wouldn't. You wouldn't."

"Convince me," said Steiner, his huge eyes glaring at me. "I got to get Varsag to do it. I'm not particular how. If that kid disappears now they'll hang it on Varsag." He turned the palms of his hands up, as if to say that he was the prisoner of circumstance. "Buzz," he said, trying to sound patient, "you got a head. Use it. You don't need a diagram to get it. You got a head."

The Professor clasped his twittery hands and waited…

HALF an hour later, Flipper and Harry drove me to the house where Dr. Varsag and Bart were staying. When I had agreed to ask Varsag to do what Steiner wanted, Steiner left the method to me, but he hadn't been prepared for my decision to go immediately. I told him why, and I was honest with him. "There's no story that I can give Dr. Varsag," I told him. "I'll have to tell him the truth."

"But he won't do it that way," Steiner thought.

"He won't do it anyway," I'd said. "All I can do is convey your threats and convince him you mean what you say."

"So what the hell do I need you for? I'll convince him faster."

"Don't bet on it. I'll do what I can. Maybe I'll sell him."

It was raining again when we left, and the roads were thick pools of mud that sucked at the wheels of our car. The house was just a little down the road, a one-story cottage to which wings had been added. When we drew near it Flipper blinked his headlights twice and stopped the car. I heard a motor start up the road and a pair of headlights switched on. A car, facing the other direction, slowly drew up to us and a man leaned out from the driver's seat. There was another man with him.

"What's up, Flipper?"

"Everything okay?"

"Sure."

Flipper turned to me. "Okay. You walk the rest of the way. If you want us to pick you up, turn the blinds in the front room twice."

I got out and walked through the rain for the twenty yards that separated the house from the road. When I drew closer I could hear the music of a symphony playing inside. The blinds were drawn. I wiped my feet on a dry, sheltered doormat and brought down the heavy brass knocker twice before the music was turned down.

Dr. Varsag opened the door. Over his shoulder, near the phonograph, I saw Bart. "Buzz Rogow! What in the name of..."

It was an hour before our conversation was through. I told him everything, just as it had happened, from the beginning. He had hired his own detectives to trace me. He had been so worried about me that if it hadn't been for Bart, he would have looked for me himself. I felt a deep, angry pain when I told him what I had brought him. He was one of the finest men I had ever met.

And when I had finished he sat quietly, thoughtfully, and asked me questions about Professor Lightfingers. And about Steiner. I told him everything I knew. His fingers drummed lightly on his knees in time with the fast last movement of the Sibelius violin concerto that Bart was playing in the next room, then he got up and went to the phone.

"It's no use," I said. "Wire's cut."

He held the phone to his ear and listened. "So it is," he said. "Thoughtful of them, but how do they expect you to get back to them?"

"We arranged a signal. They're waiting just down the road."

"Good. Will you call them, please?"

I got up. "I knew your answer from the start," I said.

The Doctor reached out and touched my arm. "Don't misquote me," he said. "You see, I mean to go through with it."

I stared at him. I couldn't understand, and then I thought of the boy in the next room. I had a lump in my throat the size of a fist.

Varsag shook his head, as if divining my thoughts. "It isn't only Bart," he said, quietly, "or you and your foolish and loyal friends. It's also me. The experiment interests me. I am offered an unusual and willing subject. There are aspects to this—"

"But you can't go through with it!"

He took off his glasses and began polishing them, and then he raised his eyes until they met mine, and I saw the profound gentleness and goodness and strength that shone in them. "Trust me, Buzz," he said, softly. "Trust me just a little."

CHAPTER FIVE

THE days that followed weren't bad at all, really. Of course I had the thing on my mind all the time, but after awhile it was more in the back of my mind than anywhere else. That was because I had confidence in Varsag. He had shouldered the whole thing himself, and once or twice when he got a chance to talk to me, he told me enough to give me a glimpse of what he was doing. Of which more in a minute.

Dr. Varsag spent most of his time with the Professor. He told him frankly that he was studying him, a requisite of the operation. The Professor enjoyed it, not only the idea, but the Doctor's company. He went for walks with Varsag all through the countryside, and evenings they played contract bridge with Swift and me, the two of them always as partners. When Varsag brought over his phonograph and records, the Professor formed a bloc with him against the others who wanted to hear Glenn Miller and racing results. They got along tremendously.

And I was the apple of Steiner's apple-size eyes. He didn't know how I had done it, but I was his boy from then on. He pounded my back so often and so heartily that I developed nervous indigestion. He trusted me completely. I took Bart back to the city in my car alone. He showed no sign of his former prowess, but he ate eggs like a normal human being again, which was more than one could say for Prager, for example. Bart spoke to me of the whole thing without much reticence, and his main concern was for the experiment that had failed, and for the way he would be received in school again. Varsag had given him letters to the Dean and several others, and Bart had a cogent and innocent story prepared, but he knew that Varsag's whereabouts were to remain a complete secret.

In the city I loaded up with all sorts of fancy food, with fowl and beef and fruit. Varsag had called his ghoulish butler on the phone in advance, and Bart helped me find the instruments and equipment the Doctor had listed for me to bring back. It went smoothly enough, though there was a brief flare-up in the papers when Bart showed up. The university, baffled itself, maintained its dignity and disclaimed everything, including notions that Varsag had done anything to Bart.

So we were quite a happy colony, the twelve of us, including the cook, Jimmy. Elmer, the Woodbourne Police Force, drove up one day and said there'd been reports of a lot of shooting in the neighborhood. We gave him a drink and showed him our target range, a bench at fifty yards with whiskey bottles on it. He took three shots himself and missed and then Pittsburg and Harry missed to make him feel better. It was the only times I'd seen them miss. Naturally, most of the colony stayed out of sight, and we bought our food miles away to forestall curiosity.

Dr. Varsag's other main occupation was his long sessions with the moles. At his request, Steiner supplied dozens of English moles, and when the Doctor wasn't observing them, he was dissecting them and making intricate diagrams and marking up his charts and notebooks. One day he lectured to the Professor and me about them.

It started when Varsag smilingly said, "So you want to be a mole, Professor? Have you thought about it much?"

The Professor produced one of Steiner's cigars. "Naturally," he said. "It isn't every day I become a mole. If I had my way, I'd sooner be a mole on Rita Hayworth's...ah...escutcheon. Can you arrange it?"

"I'm wondering if I can arrange this. Look at this little animal. Have you ever thought of it as an engineer? Yet it is undoubtedly nature's greatest engineer, far more capable in the arts of underground engineering and burrowing than any other animal, far more capable than most people imagine. It builds elaborate underground habitations, with tunnels and galleries of the most complex order, with perfect instinctive knowledge of stresses and strains, drainage, support—all the problems its work involves.

"A man who equaled the mole's mastery of its art, who did the equivalent of its burrowing, would in one night be able to dig a tunnel 37 miles long, of sufficient width to admit the passage of his body."

The Professor squinted at Varsag. "You're jesting, Doctor."

"Quite the contrary, Professor."

The Professor looked at his hands and held them up. "But how?"

VARSAG sighed. "In due time. It requires either the imagination of experience and knowledge, or the lack of imagination that our friend Steiner exercised, knowing only his goal. But in due time..."

The next day I had a chance to speak to Varsag alone.

"Doctor, it isn't that I don't trust you, but there was another time when I might have spoken and didn't, and I've regretted it since. No one knows better than you what you're doing, but isn't there a chance that your interest in your work blinds you to the possible results? If you equip a man like the Professor with such appalling ability, with Steiner to direct him..."

We were in one of the Doctor's mole fields near the house. He took my arm and led me to the road, where we started walking. "Suppose I agreed with you—which I do not," he said, "what could we do about it? Proceed calmly down this road and vanish? Call the State Police to rescue your friends? How would we explain it? Perhaps charge Steiner with abduction? He could easily establish you'd been to the city alone a few days ago. Why didn't you call the police then?"

"I'd say I was afraid for your life. You were still there."

"But your friends Swift and Prager are there now. Would you tell the police you didn't care about *them*? And remember—the assumption behind calling the police is that they could rescue anyone in time. No, I'm afraid we'd have trouble explaining, and this is no time to explain. Besides, the threat of Steiner's future revenge is quite as formidable as his threat to harm Bart. Steiner understands that as well as we do, and it explains why he let Bart go."

"Why do you say this is no time to explain?" I asked. "With Bart—"

"Because I've already begun my work on the Professor."

I stopped in my tracks. "When?"

"Two nights ago. You were asleep. Steiner was there to help me. Don't look at me like that, Buzz."

I said nothing.

Varsag sighed. "Buzz," he said, slowly, "has it occurred to you that I may really know what I'm doing? You accept the marvel of my surgical skill—though the surgery is a minute part of all this—with no thought to what else I might be able to do. If you believe I can change a man's whole internal nature so that he adopts many characteristics of an animal, why can't you believe that I might change characteristics already part of *his* nature?"

I looked at him sharply. "Change the Professor's nature?"

"Exactly."

"But in what way?"

"In many ways," said Varsag, thoughtfully, "in many ways. The mole is not a vicious animal, to begin with, and I am satisfied there is nothing vicious in the Professor's nature. Nothing *wrong*, actually, if it comes to that. Habits are not ineradicable…nor is there any reason to believe that the redirection…" He was talking more to himself now than to me, and presently his voice was so low I couldn't hear him.

We turned back silently after awhile, but when we had neared the house again, the Doctor remarked, "If you'd care to, I've a book in my room that may interest you. It deals with the subject. And you might do worse than observe the Professor. Perhaps you'll notice some results of my preliminary work." He smiled wryly. "You see, was I not satisfied with my success, I could always refuse to finish my work. I daresay you've overlooked the one indisputable escape always available to me, and with no attendant harm to anyone else."

"What?"

"Suicide," said Dr. Varsag. "Come, come, my boy, there's no danger of it, unpleasant as it sounds. All the same, I'd sooner do that than run the risk of so perilous a failure. Does that answer you?"

IT ANSWERED me, all right. After that I kept my mouth shut and my eyes open. Among other things, I noticed that the Professor had taken to eating alone, and that Steiner himself frequently went for the food, as if to keep the Professor's new diet, which I knew about, from attracting the attention of the others. But it wasn't all.

There was a change in the Professor. Or maybe not; maybe I just thought it was there because I was looking for it. Or maybe it was so slight in coming that the others didn't notice—none of them had known him except Steiner, and he said nothing. One manifestation was the Professor's increasing desire for solitude, or at least for less company. He had struck me as a very gregarious sort of person, with a constant desire to be with others, to have people listen to him and repeat his jokes and stories. But now when he was with others, he paid attention to the conversation around him, instead of concentrating on what he was going to say next.

And there was something else, as I soon discovered. He was spending much of his solitude in building things, all sorts of things. I only saw one, a large, incredibly faithful model of a battleship, with fantastically intricate installations that controlled the gun batteries and lights and anchors, complete to interior turbines. It called for the patience of a saint, and the manual dexterity of a genius, and if one was prepared to find the latter, the former was a bit surprising.

"But he's changing, my dear Buzz," Varsag explained. "His room is a workshop and museum. He's working on a model of a house of the future he read about, with enormous glass facades, mounted on a sort of swivel foundation so that the wall exposures can follow the course of the sun. He has Steiner jumping about supplying him with the necessary materials, I can tell you."

"And all this is the result of your preliminary operation?"

"Only in a limited sense. Every talented, energetic man seeks an outlet for his talent and looks for recognition. Unfortunately for humanity, as in the Professor's case, sometimes a combination of environment and other circumstances provides an outlet that is antisocial, but the drive remains. In the Professor it drove him to a fabulous eminence in his profession, a position that he made little attempt to keep a professional secret. The fame, or notoriety, you see, was what he wanted—the recognition. And among people he always tried to shine a little in other ways removed from the talent of his hands. He fancied himself a wit and rather a thinker, and wanted that recognized too."

"And now?"

"It's a little early to be absolutely sure, but it looks as if he is finding new outlets. The diet I gave him provides him with enormous energy, which, to be sure, he will need later. Meanwhile he expends it, and his ingenuity, in new creative channels. The man he might have been is emerging. When he forsakes his intellectual pretensions, as he seems to be doing, and finds adequate compensation in his skill alone, he will be a socially valuable craftsman of extraordinary skill, and quite happy in his new adjustment to society."

I began to understand. In the book I borrowed from Varsag, *"The Relation of Character to Neuro-Surgery"* by Dr. St. John Broome, R.F., F.O.S., B.A.R., I read of operational techniques that had had astounding results. There were many recorded instances of complete changes in personality, habit, disposition—all the attributes of the synthesis we call character—through the medium of surgery. The techniques ranged from removal of cerebral pressure clots to rearrangement of synapses by predetermined plan. I was amazed to discover liberal quotations from monographs by Dr. Arnold Varsag, Franz Varsag's dead brother, devoted to discussion of future possibilities in micro-neuro-surgery. Just as the various senses and other functions such as speech, memory, etc., were known to be localized in particular portions of the brain, so, he claimed, were many of the other, minor, characteristics to be found. Broome was inclined to discount many of Varsag's claims as premature, pointing out that he had not made the records of his experiments available for checking, but he agreed in principle with Varsag's direction.

IT WAS too much for me. All I knew about the brain was that it was a handy thing to have, as witness Prager's life without one. In the time we had been at Woodbourne, Swift and I, playing three-handed klobbyosch with Prager, had split some six hundred dollars of Prager's money. Our partnership was secret; the cards were marked; and Prager borrowed the money from Steiner at standard loan shark rates, a fact that made Swift and me happy, contemplating the day when he would have to cough up the borrowed moola and interest to Steiner.

So it went for perhaps another week.

There was a second midnight operation, which I found out about only because I caught a glimpse of the Professor wearing a temporary bandage in the morning. When I protested to Varsag that I resented his secrecy, he explained that he had only wanted to spare me a sight that, by its unfamiliarity alone, might have ill effects on me, but he promised that I would be present at the main operation itself.

It came toward the end of that week. The spring trout season had opened and Steiner's cutthroats, grown restive, left for two days fishing upstate, taking Prager along. Swift and I watched them leave, and Varsag, who was standing nearby, caught my questioning glance and nodded. That night we drugged Swift's and the cook's coffee, and shortly after eleven, we gathered in the Professor's room, the four of us, and helped him arrange everything for the operation. Things like sterilizing vast numbers of instruments, preparing buckets, sponges, sheets, and so on.

"I'll need your help, Buzz," Varsag said, and together with a trembling, anxious Steiner, I scrubbed my hands and donned a surgical robe. Steiner kept flitting about, talking anxiously to the Professor. He was on the last lap of his carefully nurtured relay to crime unknown, and after weeks of planning and waiting, it seemed too much for him. The

Professor was subdued, mildly interested, occasionally interposing a remark to Varsag concerning a sociological survey he had recently read. Varsag, his mind elsewhere, answered automatically while he methodically went about his business. And I? I felt like Dr. Kildare.

I regret to say that I passed out halfway through the operation. Save your snide remarks. It could happen to anyone. As it was, I lasted for more than an hour and a half; the operation took more than three.

Mostly, I checked on the ether, under Varsag's direction, and now and then dumped instruments into the sterilizer or took them out. But I sat there on a high stool, under hot, bright lights and watched a man's skull sawed open. Trepan, the Doctor called it. He took the top of the skull off like you might a hubcap, and there was the shiny, wet with blood, pink and grey convolutions of brain. Cut followed minute cut and the flashing knife went ever deeper. Not a knife really; it was more a wisp of metal, frequently invisible to the eye, directed through a series of adjustable lenses held on wheeled legs over the brain. The tip of the knife was actually invisible, except under the micro lenses.

I remember Varsag's coolness. Not a drop of perspiration was on him, though Steiner and I were drenched. I could not see his eyes because of the shaded glasses he wore, but I had no doubt they were calm and humorous as ever; he made a few jokes during the operation, which I don't remember. He worked on tirelessly, pausing for brief moments to consult his huge, illuminated charts, which hung close by, his hands in their transparent amber rubber gloves as fast and light as wind.

Somewhere around the middle I went. No particular reason, but the heat and the lights and the blood and the quiet, and, I guess, the idea of what was happening—anyway, I remember I felt the stool rocking under me and I called out,

softly, "Steiner, catch me." I came to in an adjoining room
and waited there until it was over. Varsag and Steiner carried

the Professor to his room, Varsag smiling at me and remarking that I had survived, after all. The Doctor stayed with his patient all night, and until we fell asleep downstairs on a couch, Steiner and I sat up playing double solitaire and thinking our private thoughts...

NOW the development of the Professor was swift. Change followed change with the dramatic sequence of a story. Watching him was like seeing a piece of fiction come to life, for there was something unreal in the way the changes came over him. I don't know how to describe it better. Like a man putting on a series of costumes and masks, strange masks that affected his whole bearing, that dictated his actions. Like a strip of film with Spencer Tracy turning from Jekyll to Hyde, with sudden new alterations from moment to moment. Not that they happened so quickly, but that was the impression it left.

We were more or less alone in the house now. Steiner had sent away most of his men, leaving only Flipper and Harry, and even they were not around very often. Jimmy did the cooking and Prager did the housework, content that Steiner let him stay, for his curiosity, though hidden from the others, was devouring him. Swift wanted to leave, but maybe because he asked, Steiner wouldn't let him; maybe it was his increasing case of jitters. It was like a fever that ran through the house. Some nights I would wake up for no reason and hear noises that told me that we were all awake, listening to each other, listening for we didn't know what.

A few days after the Professor was on his feet, he changed his habits from that of a daytime to a nocturnal creature. He seldom went out into the warming April sun, and then only with dark glasses, bundled in his fuzzy dark coat, walking about in the mole fields. A little past ten o'clock at night he would eat his main meal, devouring enormous quantities of heavy food. Then he would sit with us for half an hour and retire to his room. Sometimes we would hear him working on the small lathe Steiner had installed for him, sometimes we would hear him patting down the hallway to get a drink, his footsteps soft and hurried. In the morning there would be minute shavings of metal that had fallen from his clothes to the upstairs hallway floor, so small that you knew they were there only because they crunched under your feet.

Then he began quarreling violently with Jimmy, the cook. If his food wasn't ready when he wanted it, or if it wasn't prepared exactly as he liked, he flew into a rage, shouting and screaming curses. Varsag understood it and told us that it was a peculiarity of the mole, serving to replace an outlet for the enormous energy he had developed, and which he might have put into his burrowing.

No one mentioned that. There was some silent understanding among us not to bring up the subject of this most natural, this great, instinctive drive of the mole, not even among ourselves. But we were all waiting for it. The expectancy lay in our minds like a dormant animal, a fierce but patient thing, waiting to seize the first sign of the beginning of the final stage.

One afternoon I walked into the kitchen and found the refrigerator open, and a trail of wet drippings, like a mixture of water and beef blood, leading to the cellar door. I had assumed the Professor was asleep upstairs, but with three pounds of beef gone, the indication was too clear to mistake. Not wanting to embarrass him, for he insisted on eating alone, but still curious about his taking beef to the cellar, I quietly went around to the back and looked into the cellar through one of the little windows.

The sun was shining directly down through the window. I might not have noticed the Professor at first, for he was sitting in the darkness of a corner, but the meat lay on a paper bag, and part of the bag projected into the sunlit area. The bag moved, and I strained my eyes and saw the Professor's hands tearing the meat. He was eating it raw! I must have made some slight noise, otherwise he would never have turned and forced himself to look up into the sunlight. His incredibly developed sense of hearing caught whatever imperceptible sound I made, and he thrust his head out from behind the shelter of a pile of boxes.

AT FIRST his eyes were closed. His mute, taut face was turned to me, and then slowly he opened his eyes to mere slits and he saw me. He jumped to his feet with a cry of rage and threw the meat at the window with such force that it shattered, the splinters cutting my hand as I instinctively threw them up. I drew back and he was gone.

Varsag and Steiner, who were on the front porch, came running. Varsag cleaned the cuts as I told him what had happened. He said nothing, but later he warned both Steiner and me against provoking him. His fits of anger would pass soon, the Doctor said. He was beginning to eat even during the day, storing the energy he would soon call into play.

We made no attempt to find him, but that night when the Professor came downstairs for his dinner, as he walked through the living room to the kitchen, he stopped a moment before me. We had turned down all but one lamp when we heard him coming, but he still wore his dark glasses.

"I'm sorry about this afternoon," he said to me, his voice very low. "I'm really dreadfully sorry. I hope you weren't hurt."

When I reassured him, he went into the kitchen and we could hear him talking quite civilly to Jimmy. Jimmy soon left, and when the Professor finished eating, he came into the living room and sat down. In a gesture of politeness he removed his glasses, shielding his eyes with a hand. He seemed rested and at ease.

"Well, Professor," said Varsag, cordially, "how is it today?"

"Better, much better, thank you," the Professor sighed. "I keep wondering about your operation, however. For a mole, I eat like a tiger and I've the vision of a bat. I was thinking that if you'd changed me into a porcupine, I could make love to a cactus plant and never know the difference. Unless," he added, laughing softly, "I ate it first."

My first reaction to his words was shock. After such careful avoidance of the subject with him, to hear him actually joking about it was startling and almost obscene. Steiner, too, seemed to have reacted as I had, but not Varsag. The Doctor cocked an amused eyebrow and a little smile played on his lips. "And your hearing?" he asked. "Don't you find that it compensates a good deal for your diminished vision?"

"It interferes with my sleep."

"You mean we make too much noise during the afternoon?"

"That depends on what you call too much noise," said the Professor. "This afternoon Swift woke me when he went to the upstairs bathroom."

Swift, sitting in a chair near the radio, sat up. "I beg your pardon," he objected. "I did nothing but comb my hair."

"That's it exactly," said the Professor, slyly. "You're losing your hair. I could hear them falling to the floor, like hailstones."

Steiner let out a howl and I couldn't help laughing myself. It drained me of all the tension that that day had brought, and though it lasted for an instant, I was grateful. But for all the Professor's light-hearted banter, his face was tightening again, and his feet were beating a swift, nervous tattoo under his chair.

"What about other things?" Varsag asked. "Surely there have been other manifestations natural to your new state?"

The Professor let his hands down and peered at Varsag, thrusting his face forward. He pointed a long, dirty finger at the Doctor and said, "Ah, Doctor, who's doing the digging now?" He bounded to his feet as if he had released a spring, and bidding us all goodnight, he ran upstairs with a series of throaty chuckles trailing behind him.

Presently, Steiner said, "Well, Doc? Well? Does it figure?"

Varsag shrugged and sat thoughtfully for a long time. Soon we could hear the Professor's lathe spinning furiously. Swift turned the radio on low and after awhile one of our interminable card games began.

WE HAD been at it perhaps half an hour when the door opened and Prager came running in. He had been to the village to get some bottled beer, and he stood there, surveying us stupidly, the half case of beer on his shoulder. He looked at us again and put the case down, as if he had been on the verge of saying something and changed his mind.

"For crying out loud!" Steiner exploded. "Say it, will you?"

"Nothing," said Prager. "When I seen the Professor in the village, I thought maybe you didn't know he—"

"You saw *who* in the village?" Steiner cried.

"The Professor. You mean you didn't know he was there?"

Steiner leaped up and ran up the stairs, with Varsag and me just behind him. He tried to open the Professor's door, but it was locked. From inside the Professor called, sharply, "What do you want?"

We stood there and as we heard the lathe whir to a stop, it occurred to all of us that we had heard the lathe all the time under the music of the radio. Steiner's face turned from astonishment to fury, but he kept his voice controlled. "You want some beer?" he asked.

"No." The lathe started again.

We went downstairs and Steiner took Prager by the lapels. "Where did you see him—in the bar you stopped in for a quick one?"

"That's it," Prager gulped. "I had just one. I swear I—"

Dr. Varsag caught Steiner's hand before it could land. "None of that, please," he said. "The mistake was innocent enough. It isn't the boy's fault if our reactions are somewhat exaggerated." He took Prager by the arm and led him outside. They spoke together for a minute or so, and then we heard them go walking down the road, still talking.

Steiner looked at me. "What the hell goes on here?" he said.

"Pixies," said Swift, sarcastically, and as Steiner took a step toward him, he reached for a poker and said, "You lay one of your hairy arms on me and I'll have your damn mole-man dig you a grave."

Steiner stopped dead in his tracks and turned to me again. "The whole house is crazy," he said, solemnly. "Pixies is just the half of it." He sank back to his chair and shuffled the cards. "The whole house is crazy, crazy, crazy," he mumbled. "My deal."

The lathe was still spinning when we went up to bed an hour later. Dr. Varsag and Prager hadn't returned.

CHAPTER SIX

I WOKE to find Prager standing beside my bed, shaking me gently. He turned on the night lamp and I saw that it was five past three on my clock. In the next bed, Swift sat up, blinking in the light.

Prager put a finger to his lips.

"Shhh," he cautioned. "Get up or you'll miss it. The Professor's gone. He dug a hole out of the cellar and he's in it somewhere. Come on."

"I hear the lathe still going," said Swift.

Prager screwed his face up wisely and winked. "That's it. He used the lathe as a blind. I told you I saw him in the village."

I got into my robe and slippers and followed Prager into the hallway. Swift behind us. Prager tiptoed to the Professor's door and pushed it open, whispering that he had picked the lock. A tiny light, dimmed by towels draped over the lampshade, showed us the unattended lathe still spinning away. The room was a mess, littered with scrap.

Cautiously, we went downstairs. I opened the cellar door and saw Varsag sitting on a box, with a couple of candles to provide a light. The Doctor scowled when he saw us. "I distinctly told you not to wake anyone," he said to Prager. "Now you'll all sneak back to bed. I can't have you here without Steiner. He'd be furious if he—"

All our heads turned together. We all heard the distant noise, like something scurrying, but with a hollow, far off sound. Varsag took one of the candles and moved it toward the nearest wall and I sucked in my breath. For behind the pile of boxes where I had seen the Professor that afternoon, there was a large mound of fresh earth, and just beyond it, a hole that gaped in the foundation wall and dipped away, a hole with a diameter of some thirty inches!

"Quick! Get Steiner!" the Professor ordered. "Before he comes!"

Prager backed away, his eyes on the hole, and ran upstairs.

I just couldn't believe it. "But how could he get through such blocks of concrete?" I breathed. "The stones...the concrete..."

Varsag nodded, his face thoughtful.

"You forget this is not just a mole," he said softly. "This is a trained, cunning, superior human intelligence combined with the greatest natural burrowing instinct known. The combination is more than a match for anything mankind can produce." He moved the candle closer to the edge of the hole. The stone showed evidence of great scratches, as if it had been torn apart by fantastic claws, by something beyond our understanding.

A MOMENT later, Steiner came running down the stairs. He was barefoot and in his underwear, and he looked baffled and angry. He was about to say something when Dr. Varsag held up a hand. The hollow sound had echoed once more. Closer and closer the clawing, scraping noises approached, increasing in intensity, then suddenly they stopped. Long moments of utter silence went by, until Varsag muttered. "Perhaps he's afraid to come out because the light—"

At that moment several chunks of concrete from the opposite wall fell to the cellar floor. We turned in time to see the rest of the new hole being punched through, catching a glimpse of something that gleamed like dark blue metal as it whirred in a shower of sparks. Then quiet, and a moment later the Professor's head popped out add quickly drew back again. He was exercising the mole's caution about exits and entrances!

We watched the hole until the Professor's head appeared again. He looked out at us, his dirt-blackened face creased in a furtive but very friendly smile, and then he crawled out on all fours and stood up, arching his back and grunting amiably. He kept looking at us, still smiling, in the oddest mixture of pride and shyness, then he stroked his lips with a forefinger and asked, "Who found me? Come now, who found me out? I've a reward for him, you see."

I don't think he understood then why none of us could speak. For he was clad in a suit made of carefully sewn moleskins, reinforced with several thicknesses at the knees and elbows. Over his shoulders hung two long moleskin bags, both so heavy that they kept him bowed. In the one that hung down over his chest he had swiftly stowed the gleaming, claw-like tools we had glimpsed. Now he swung the other bag around and I swear I saw his ears move at the jingling sound the bag made, and he dug a hand into the bag.

"I know, I know," he said, slyly, pointing his finger at Prager and smiling. "It was you—so here!"

And when he opened the fist of his other hand, a shower of gold coins fell to the cellar floor, glistening with a dull, yellow brilliance in the candlelight.

I'll never forget the look that was on Varsag's face...

OF COURSE, Varsag was wrong. We all were—then. Remembering how the Doctor was later to say to Steiner, "He's yours now, whatever you plan to do with him..." and remembering that we all had the same ideas about those plans, I realize that even at the beginning our thought was instantaneous and identical. And wrong.

The Professor had found the coins buried in a box in a nearby field. It lay in the path of the tunnel he dug to the village. The tunnel exited on the banks of a small local river; it was one of the Professor's earliest underground explorations, and he made use of it by going into the village bar. He liked to think that there was some useful purpose served by his work. It was something he had read in his borrowed books on economics—production for use—so he dug a magnificent tunnel nearly two miles long and used it as a private road to get a beer!

Oh, we found out a lot about him before Steiner took him over. He privately showed Varsag and Steiner the tools he had made, and Varsag described them to me with awe in his voice, but I didn't understand. He had fashioned high-test steel and various alloys into an array of miraculous tools, drills and torches so compact, so wonderful and unbelievable in their design and efficiency that even Varsag had not expected so prodigious a success. For this being of mole and man had developed a kind of mind that was beyond our comprehension.

I was there the afternoon he showed Dr. Varsag one of the tools in operation. He took his moleskin bag into a field, and from it he took out a pair of metal gloves—if I may call it that—which reached almost to his shoulders. An interior switch turned on a tiny motor, and four, curved talon-like spades began spinning with such speed that they were mere blurs. At the same time, flat, triangular sections of steel that reached from wrist to elbow began a powerful motion all their own, designed to pack the loose, dug up soil to either side of the swift blades. It seemed inconceivable that this instrument—but what's the use of talking about it? The Professor bent over and touched the ground. The spring hay flew aside in a hail of earth...

In a quarter of a minute the Professor was gone, and where he had been there was a small mound of fresh, wet earth and a hole that was two feet deep before it curved parallel to the ground surface. A minute later, seventy-five yards away, the Professor came out of the ground and waved to us.

"It saves the wear and tear on our fingernails," he said later.

That was another thing about him, that use of the first person plural, like royalty, or newspaper columnists; take your pick. There was a strong, if sly, pride in his voice whenever he spoke of his feats, as if the entire responsibility for his achievements was his. And yet, he was closer to Varsag than anyone else.

It was Varsag, for instance, that he told of his plan to dig a tunnel into the Museum of Modern Art, or the Natural History Museum—he wasn't sure which. He wanted to burrow down the length of the state, under the Hudson, then downtown like a damn one-man subway and get in through the Museum cellar. Why? To make them an anonymous present of his battleship and glass house models. "They would be useful," he said the Doctor told me later.

He also told Steiner, and that ended the plan. Varsag had pointed out that the gift could be made via Railway Express, and that a tunnel into the cellar of a museum could hardly be enthusiastically received by the authorities. "But I would block off the tunnels later," the Professor explained. "They'd never know I got in through a tunnel." Steiner listened and observed that he had better uses for such energy and ingenuity and the subject seemed closed, though we all remembered the box and the coins.

THERE was some eight thousand dollars in gold in that box. It had been buried three feet underground, on land that belonged to the owner of the house Steiner had rented. But since none of the coins bore a date more recent than 1901, and since the box itself was lined with a newspaper from 1903, it seemed safe to assume that the gold had belonged to someone long dead. At any rate, Steiner would have confiscated it, if the Professor had not stolen it from him and buried it again, or said he had buried it again. We didn't know for sure, the way he spoke.

We had a nasty half hour the morning Steiner found the gold was missing, until the Professor woke up and confessed. "I want it," he said. "Gold is useful. I will find a use for it." So Steiner, with other things on his mind, shrugged it off, and the Professor went back to sleep. In the cellar. He wouldn't sleep in a bed anymore. He made himself a bed from bits of felt and crumpled newspapers and burlap and he slept in the cellar, just inside one of his tunnels.

It took a little while for us to grow accustomed to him, and all that time we knew that Steiner was getting ready to take over, and we were waiting. Steiner was as earnest a student of the Professor as Dr. Varsag. He learned the more simple peculiarities of the Professor's mind. It had changed, you see, in many ways. It had become more simple and more direct, for one. If the Professor wanted to deceive someone, he didn't lie or dissemble—he just kept his mouth shut and then did what he wanted to do. Where he had been cynical before, he was now sly, in an animal way; where he had been sophisticated before, he was now wary. And though he was in many ways independent, he developed a need for discussion about himself and about matters pertaining to him.

Varsag patiently explained everything. When one of the Professor's tools betrayed him one day, and he bored through into an underground stream that flooded his tunnel and almost drowned him before he escaped, Varsag reassured him that it was not his judgment that had been at fault. He explained his past rages, now very rare, and explained why the Professor's hearing was so acute, and numerous other minor matters.

Day after day, night after night, with only brief intervals for sleeping and feeding, the Professor perfected his tools. During this time he constructed an elaborate series of underground chambers, and at the Doctor's request, he enlarged some of his tunnels and chambers so that Varsag himself was able to crawl down into them. It was a great concession, and when he offered me the opportunity to go down, I was at once overwhelmed and very grateful.

What can I say that would give you an idea of what it was like? It was like being an underground animal. It was a glimpse into the life of something so alien, so far removed even from the imagination of a normal human, that I left his chambers cool with fear. They were marvels of engineering, perfectly ventilated and drained, with innumerable side galleries running off to unknown places, with a dozen exits and entrances and caches of food and drink to appease his enormous needs. Swift and Prager were with me, and it affected them much the same.

IT was that same day that Steiner made his first move toward beginning his own plans. If he had been disturbed by the Professor's increasing closeness to Varsag, this new display of friendship for the rest of us was the finishing touch. And, having also seen what the Professor was now capable of doing, he thought his time had arrived. Dr. Varsag agreed. He had been on the verge of making the same point.

"My work with him is finished now," he said. "He's yours now, whatever you plan to do with him. But only upon one condition; that if and when the time arrives that you are through with him, when you have no further use for him, you will allow him to return to me."

Whatever Steiner thought of this strange condition, he accepted it. He was a different Steiner. I knew that, and knew that it was due to the weeks he had lived with Varsag. You can't live with a man like that and not change in some ways. He had learned what it was to respect a man for himself, for his ability, for his opinions, for his word, and not for the gun he carried, or the men he could hire to kill you.

The old Steiner might never have let us leave that farm alive, once he had what he wanted. The thought had been with me several times, but Varsag had brushed it aside when I spoke of it. And he had been right. The new—or slightly altered—Steiner not only let us go, but provided other surprises. He took the Doctor's word for his responsibility that nothing of what had been done there would be revealed by any of us. In parting, he gave Swift and Prager five thousand dollars each, to compensate them for their semi-captivity and bribe them to a silence, which Varsag's word had already bound them to keep.

I don't know what he offered Varsag, but Varsag didn't accept it. He told me to keep whatever remained of the money he had given me. I had drawn against it both for him and myself, leaving some fourteen thousand dollars. At the end of the month, when my bank forwarded its statement, I discovered that either he or Swift's pixies had deposited exactly enough to bring my balance to an even fifty thousand dollars. The generosity behind that action floored me, but that was because the month ended a week or so after we left, and it was a few days before I understood his motives. Generous, yes. But he thought he could afford it by then.

Somehow, it was a sad business, that leaving. The Professor was asleep, and Steiner wouldn't let us wake him to say goodbye. It was the end of April. The wind blew through the bright, fresh green of the fields, and birds circled in the sunlight. The countryside was quiet and at rest. We were all tanned and in better health than some of us had been in a long time. When, just before we left, Flipper and Harry drove up to the house on one of their rare visits—Steiner had sent them to the house down the road to live the last few weeks—it forcibly reminded us that the business that had kept us there had not been meant for our health.

As we drove away, Varsag, beside me, said quietly, "And now we will wait. How long will it be…?"

I DIDN'T know what he meant, but when I finally did, it was some days later—just about ten days. The headline was just a double column on the bottom of the first page, but the story was interesting:

MERCHANTS TRUST CO. BANK ROBBED.
LOOT ESTIMATED AT NEAR $100,000

Scientific Burglars Dig Tunnels
From Vacant Store on Same Block

NEW YORK, MAY 4 (UP) .—A crew of burglars with the patience of saints and the conscientious precision of engineers robbed the Merchants' Trust Co. Bank Canal Street Branch of almost $100,000.00 yesterday, between the hours of closing and opening. Police officials who quickly traced the robbers' path stated that the robbery had been carefully planned and executed with supreme skill and efficiency.

Starting from their concealed headquarters in a vacant store at 5518 Canal Street, the burglar spent weeks carefully burrowing a tunnel for some hundred yards and passed under several other stores before they pointed their drills and torches upward. There they met blocks of concrete and vault steel, but neither of these…

And so on, as you may remember—I won't bore you with it. The police were amazed, were investigating storeowners and patrolmen, were at a loss to explain, were assigning detectives. No fingerprints, no clues, nothing—nothing but two feet of porous concrete and eight inches of ventilated steel, and a tunnel straight as an arrow. Big things expected to develop momentarily, however. What a laugh!

I was at Varsag's house half an hour after I saw the papers. He had seen them already. He invited me to share his late breakfast, his voice subdued, his manner reflective. I sat there sipping coffee, waiting for him to say something. He let me wait until he had finished the last of a mountain of marmaladed toast.

"Well, my boy?" he said. "You're upset, aren't you? You're sure this is the Professor's work."

"Aren't you?"

"Half and half," he said, taking one of my cigarettes. "It might just be a coincidence. However, I am ready to accept the alternative that it was Professor Lightfingers."

Slowly, I said, "Then you think...you failed?"

He tapped the newspaper. "Does that sound like failure?"

That startled me. "You know what I mean, sir," I said.

"What would you have me do? Shall I call in the police and tell them I think Professor Williams dug that tunnel because of an operation I performed on him?"

"No, not that, exactly..."

"Then what, exactly?"

"I—I don't know. Maybe all I wanted to hear was that you're worried...that you..." I think I must have been staring at him.

"That I am about to take poison, perhaps?" He snorted impatiently. "Certainly not. Failure? Certainly not. You can't expect a man to shed the habits of a lifetime like a coat. If you broke your leg, you wouldn't expect to walk the moment it was set in a cast?" He got up and came around to me, putting a hand on my arm. "But it's not him you were thinking about, was it? You really were worried about me. You're a good lad, Buzz. I appreciate your concern. As for this story, let's wait until we have something more we can go by."

SO that was the way we left it. I didn't understand something in the Doctor's attitude, but I tried not to let it bother me. But a guy like me, used to feeling little things like that, the intangibles in a conversation, in a glance, in the tone of a voice—a guy like that can't just keep blinking. Something more to go by? We got those somethings more, plenty of them, in the next few days.

On May fifth, the Farmers' Exchange Bank on Fiftieth and Broadway was burglarized to the merry tune of $160,000, with two-foot holes in steel walls and no tunnels. On May 7th, the Bronx County Bank lost $70,000, with several small tunnels. On May 10th, the Highland Trust Co. was robbed of $210,000, with one tunnel nearly three hundred yards long, and drainage arranged for Miller Creek, which was near the tunnel. By May 18th, ten banks had lost close to a million and a half dollars.

No peanuts, brother. The police went crazy. They raided every hangout and fence and hotshop in town, and the FBI came in because of the Federal Reserve Banks included. The newspapers turned out editorials you could hear sizzling. Weeks of preparation, like they'd said at the first robbery? Hah! If that was true, there were six hundred skilled eggs operating around New York, and that was a bigger and crazier crime syndicate than even the movies dreamed about. So what was the answer? They had runs on a dozen or so banks. What was the answer?

Steiner could have told them, but Steiner wasn't around, Varsag knew, but he had disappeared. He'd been gone for days, ever since that first robbery. He came in once and I got him on the phone, but he was in a hurry and couldn't talk to me. "Don't worry and whatever you do, don't say anything about it," he told me, and hung up. I guess the cops must have thought of the Professor long before, but where were they going to find him?

Then, late one night, Steiner came to my place. A crazy, wild-eyed Steiner, alone. When I opened the door he ran in and grabbed my arms and kept saying, "You've got to find him for me, Buzz! You've got to find him before I go out of my head!" He was trembling like a leaf.

I sat him down and poured him a stiff drink. He hadn't shaved in days, his shirt was dirty, and he had deep, hollow rings under his eyes. When he'd steadied a bit, I asked him who I had to find for him.

"The Doc! His butler keeps telling me he's out of town!"

"I don't know where he is. Why do you want him?"

"It's the Professor! I can't stop him! He's knocking off every bank in New York and burying the money someplace! I can't stop him and I can't get the money and I can't find Varsag! You got to find him!"

That almost floored me. I took a drink myself, and gradually I got the story out of him. He had brought the Professor closer to the city, at East Islip, Long Island. After a few days, during which he got up a list of banks and informative details about them, he had let the Professor try his hand. The first one had been out on the Island. It hadn't attracted too much attention from the New York papers, for several reasons. One was the comparatively small take—$35,000, or just about what Steiner had added to my bank balance—and second, the job had been done with a minimum of damage, and all tunnels well concealed.

The robberies we knew about had followed. The Professor had dug tunnels into the city like traffic arteries, and night after night he plundered banks. But he never returned with any of the money, and he refused to tell Steiner what he had done with it.

"A million and a half!" Steiner groaned, his great eyes wild at the thought. "I never saw a cent of it. He keeps burying the money!"

He had tried to confine the Professor, but he might as well have tried to bottle a plague. The Professor turned the house into a Swiss cheese. His tools were secreted everywhere, and he dug through floors and walls, and when he reached his hidden caches he picked up his other tools. He had exhausted Steiner's list, and then, from the way he went at other banks, he must have torn a new list out of the 'Red Book.'

STEINER had never killed a man himself—he had always hired his executioners—but three nights before he came to see me, he had resolved to kill the Professor the next time he saw him! He saw him that very night, but in the interim something new and terrible had happened, something Steiner had tried to stave off. His men, now left out of what was going on, nevertheless knew enough to guess close to the truth. They had descended on him, accusing him of holding out on the colossal fortune he was reaping. In vain his story, his pleading. He had taken his last opportunity to escape and broken away from them that night.

He had run through the fields to one of the Professor's exits he knew about, and he had waited there until dawn, when the Professor found him. And there he had pleaded with the Professor to hide him.

For two days and nights, Steiner the mighty had lived in an underground chamber, sleeping on rags, eating whatever garbage the Professor brought back from his forages, content with the leftovers. And finally, sick and feverish from exposure, half starved, frightened out of his wits, he had gotten up courage enough to sneak into the city to seek out Varsag. Now that Varsag's butler had told him the Doctor was out of town, he had come to me in desperation, not knowing where else to turn. The great Steiner, his clothes thick with mud and evil-smelling, his heavy lips quivering, his eyes searching every corner.

"Help me, Buzz," he begged. "I was good to you when I had it. Get to Varsag and call the Professor off. Help me…"

I was afraid to keep him at my place, so I got a cab and took him to Swift's home. We let him shower and fed him, and after reassuring him, we gave him some sleeping tablets and he finally dozed off. And then I told Swift everything that had happened. He hadn't asked a single question when I brought Steiner in.

When I was through, he looked at me without saying anything and went over to his phone and dialed a number. "Hello," he said. "This is Larry. Buzz Rogow is here. Something's up. Come over right away." He hung up and as he walked back to me, he said, "Varsag never left town. He's been in his house ever since we got back from Woodbourne, and he's been seeing the Professor almost every day."

It didn't make sense. It was insane. He was wrong.

He shook his head. "Funny," he said, with a tight, bitter smile. "Here I've been going along, reconciled to the fact that I'm one of the largest Simple Simons in modern history, and at this late date I find my rivals in such clever lads like Steiner and you. Am I the reincarnation of Sherlock Holmes, or what? Hasn't the solution impressed you as elementary, Buzz Watson?"

"Forget the stylish speeches. What is it?"

"Varsag's got the money."

"You're crazy!"

"Why?"

"Because—because Varsag's not that kind of man! What makes you say a thing like that? How do you know Varsag's home? How do you know he sees the Professor?"

"That was Prager I just phoned," said Swift. "Suspicious, curious Prager, who's been haunting Varsag's house since we got back, who's shadowed everyone who went in or out of that house—just one person, Meadows, the butler. Meadows takes a cab downtown every day to the West Side Receiving Market. He buys on an average of ten pounds of meat a day. For whom? For himself? For his pet canary? For the Doctor's animals? That food arrives in a truck, twice a week. It isn't choice beef or the best steaks money can buy. Who eats that food? Who in this whole wide crazy world eats like that except the Professor? And is the Professor coming to Varsag's house—I don't know how, but probably through his tunnels—does he come there to chat with the butler? Is there the slightest shred of evidence except the butler's word, that Varsag ever did leave town?"

HE stood at the window, waiting for me to speak, and when I was silent, he went on. "After all, none of us knew exactly what Varsag was doing to the Professor. They were together constantly. Even Steiner got to be afraid of their friendship, and the Professor's great dependence on Varsag. I had my ideas, but I kept quiet about them. When Stash turned up with his news a couple of weeks ago, I wondered about it but I still kept quiet, not knowing what to make of it. But this, what you've just told me, this really makes sense. It's one plus one, minus Steiner, and it adds up to Varsag getting everything. Figure it out."

I figured, but I couldn't get it. I was like a guy with a hard problem, with elements he couldn't understand, but who had the answer and was trying to force his inadequate figures to give him the answer he already knew. Because I had the answer, you see. I knew, with the complete certainty of, say—if you can stand another image, I was as certain as a sleepwalker is of his footing—that Varsag had done no such thing. I started with the premise that Varsag was honest and decent and incapable of such an action, not with the facts, whatever they were. If the facts didn't supply my answer, the facts were wrong.

I said so even after Prager arrived and substantiated everything Swift had told me. Maybe Varsag was home and had been there all along. There was still an honest answer. The facts were misleading.

"You remind me of something funny," Swift said. "You remember the Marx brothers in 'A Day at the Races,' I think it was? Groucho is a horse doctor and a woman comes to him with her x-rays. He tells her that her leg is broken, and she waves the x-rays in his face and shouts that the x-rays show something entirely different. Groucho, completely at ease, haughtily says to her: 'Madam, who are you going to believe—me, or those crooked x-rays?' And that's what you're saying, Buzz."

I picked up my hat. "If I know Groucho," I said, "that woman had a broken leg."

"Where are you going?"

"To Varsag."

"Wait for us!" Prager screamed. "Remember, I told you!"

CHAPTER SEVEN

IT was past two o'clock in the morning when we got there. I rang the bell for a minute before the little door window opened and Meadows' face appeared framed in it. Before he could say a word, I reached in and grabbed his under lip with my thumb and forefinger and pulled on it. "Open the door," I said. He opened it.

We slammed the door into him and knocked him against the wall.

"Where is Dr. Varsag?" I said.

For all his size and macabre appearance, Meadows was a lamb. He was frightened stiff. "In the study, sir, expecting you," he gasped, "but these other gentlemen—"

"We're no gentlemen," said Prager, gruffly. "Stand aside..."

"Did you say the Doctor was expecting me?" I said.

A door opened down the length of the dimly lit foyer and light poured out of the study, outlining Dr. Varsag as he stood there. "Didn't you get my message, Buzz?" said the Doctor, coming toward us. "I telephoned you several times hours ago, and then I called your building and left word for you with the doormen." He looked at us and at Meadows, saying, "But if you didn't get my message, why did..." He broke off there, sensing what was wrong, seeing the coldness on Swift and Prager, seeing how frightened Meadows was. "Come into my study, gentlemen," he said, leading the way.

When we were all settled, the Doctor asked, "What is it?"

I started to tell him, but even at the start I knew I had been right, and it made talking difficult. I told him about Steiner and what Prager had told us, and all the time I kept trying to make it sound as if it wasn't suspicion or mistrust that had brought us there—as certainly it wasn't in my case. I tried to tell him that we had come precisely because we knew there was an answer, and that he would tell us if he thought it necessary, and that Steiner's predicament had been the chief cause of our coming.

I didn't fool him. He listened to me gravely, tugging at his beard, playing with his glasses, occasionally letting his eyes wander from one to another of us, and when I was through, I knew he had it all worked out in his mind. I had seldom been as grateful to his intelligence and acumen as I was then; it would have hurt me deeply if I had thought he believed me guilty of entertaining such thoughts about him.

"I see," he said, quietly. "I'm glad you're all here. We've been in this thing together all along, and it's fitting we should be together in it now. As a matter of fact, it was my intention to send for you as soon as Buzz got here." He hesitated a moment, then said, "The truth is, gentlemen, that I've preferred not to be at home to callers precisely because the Professor has been coming here—and because I do have the money the Professor has stolen these past weeks."

Complete silence followed. I then met Varsag's gaze momentarily. His eyes were clouded, his face sober and careworn. He was fully dressed, I had noticed, though it was long past his usual bedtime. After a moment he began to speak again, his voice as calm as before. For the first time, Prager and Swift heard of the previous operations Dr. Varsag had performed on the Professor, the ones calculated to change his habits and personality.

"That my work was successful then, I had no doubt, nor do I doubt it now. I never believed it was possible to achieve a complete change in him from the outset; that would have been foolish. I did believe that I could produce enough of a change in him, even from the beginning, that for all the persistence of his past activities and the influence of Steiner's direction, he would not be dangerous to society during the period of his acclimation to his new personality and interests, as well as his new abilities.

"With that in mind, I first won his friendship and respect. I lent him books to read, and had long discussions with him, and he was fertile ground. From the very beginning, his inclinations changed. He became interested in helping society, instead of attacking it. He built a model house and wanted to present it to a museum. When he discovered a buried hoard, he refused to give it to Steiner, but hid it again until such time as I could safely take it in my luggage when we left.   His first thought was always to find some constructive use for what he was able to do.   It still is—"

"What's constructive about knocking off banks?" said Prager.

VARSAG shook his head. "Nothing, of course. I'm glad to see that you agree with the rest of society about that, Prager, but unfortunately, the Professor doesn't.   For two reasons. The first is that he has been reading things that are really too much for him.   His simple, direct mind cannot fathom most of the works of economics he's read.   He isn't equipped—now, more than ever—to deal with abstractions. A discussion about the necessity to produce for the good of society leaves him with vague notions and a slogan.   He thinks these things out, and he is conscious of his power, and he decides to do something.   Somewhere, it seems, he read of idle capital lying in banks, contributing nothing to the general welfare—"

Swift interrupted.   "Dr Varsag, are you trying to tell us that he's been stealing money to keep it from being idle?"

"Exactly.   He planned to distribute the money as soon as he stole it.   Not with any very definite plan, I'm afraid.   He told me he would give it to the poor, in person, perhaps, or by mailing it to charitable organizations.   He wanted to build hospitals, cooperatives, factories run by the workers.   I knew it would be useless to try to reason him out of trying to achieve these commendable ideals with stolen money, so my emphasis was on practical difficulties.   I took him out one night and let him give a man a ten-dollar bill.   The reaction— the man threw the money down and yelled for the police— convinced him.   I told him that charities would react the same way.   And I pointed out that building hospitals and factories called for many times the money he had.

"You may say I was thus encouraging him to go on robbing, and from a legal point of view you are right. But there are other aspects. The Professor is an incredibly valuable human to society, or will be when he stops his marauding. That he will stop I am positive, absolutely positive. He is still acting on vestigial impulses from a former self that never hesitated to rob, and his present muddled self has not helped him much. But his instincts are fundamentally sound. You know he never brought a cent of his loot to Steiner. He brought it all to me, because he trusts me, because I have said I will help him distribute his money.

"I have every dollar he has stolen. It is safely hidden in this house, waiting for the day when the Professor emerges fully as a new being. That day I will return all of it, taking the full responsibility upon myself for everything he has done.

"You may remember the agreement I made with Steiner—that if the time came that he was through with the Professor, he would allow him to return to me. I had no expectation then that he would come to me from the beginning, though I foresaw Steiner's difficulties. From what you've told me, Steiner thought of killing the Professor first, but it does not matter. He has now given me the Professor of his own will...at a time most critical...most dangerous..."

As the Doctor finished speaking, his voice dying away, the total effect of his words had been so great that none of us at first paid too much attention to his last, few words. There was just a vast quiet.

Presently Swift said to me, faintly, "Buzz, that woman should have listened to Groucho."

I was looking at Varsag. He didn't seem to be listening to us.

"Doctor," I said, "you said this was a dangerous time. Is there something you haven't told us? Something connected, perhaps, with the coincidence that you sent for me earlier—"

Varsag put a finger to his lips, silencing me. I too had heard the sound, a light tap-tap-tapping with a metallic ring. Varsag walked over to the radiator and tapped a letter-opener on it in answer. Then he came back to us and said, "It's the Professor. He's in the cellar, and now that I've answered him, he'll be up directly. You'll see what I was about to tell you."

THE Doctor turned down half the lights and we waited. Half a minute later, the great study door slowly swung open and the Professor's head popped into the room and popped right out again. Ten seconds later he repeated the process, and then slowly, in response to Varsag's call for him to come in, he let his head past the door, looked at us, then came in with two or three nimble steps, softly closed the door and kept looking at us.

"Hello!" he said brightly. "Hello! Hello! I'm glad to see all of you. Glad to find you here. News for you—dear Ira's disappeared! Left him in a nest last night—this morning?—tonight? Can't tell time much these days. All the same down under. Gone when I got back. Disappeared! Had a horrible lot of food for him, too."

Then he unslung the several moleskin bags that hung from his shoulders, weighing him down, and placed them gently on the Oriental rug. He stuck his hand into one of the bags and began piling up a small hill of currency, humming a little tune as he worked. He was wearing his dark glasses and the moleskin suit, which was utterly bedraggled, and he had forsaken his shoes somewhere, wearing pointed elfin, soft sandals. When he had taken out all the money in the bag, he took two handfuls of packaged currency and came to us.

"Here!" he said, throwing the money to us. "Use it wisely! Use it. Don't let it lie around. Do good with it!" He grinned at our bewilderment. "Wouldn't have given it to you another night. Had to save it all, let it pile up until there was a lot, then do what I wanted. But not now. All the money I want now. Just go and take it."

I caught Varsag's slight motion and the nodding of his head, telling me to draw the Professor out.

"All the money you want?" I said. "Where is it?"

"Fort Knox, Kentucky."

"WHAT?" I shrieked. "WHAT DID YOU SAY?"

I almost blew him off his feet. He jumped back and lowered his chin to his chest, eyeing us carefully. "Fort Knox!" he said quickly.

"Butbutbutbutbut why? Whatwhatwhat do you want from FORT KNOX?"

"Don't you know there's money there? Twenty billion in gold!"

I took a firm hold of myself right then and there. I was just saying absurd things, asking absurd questions. I dug Swift's arm out of my stomach and helped Prager off the floor back to the couch. We all held hands and breathed deeply in unison, the Professor regarding us in mild astonishment. When I thought my hands were steady enough, I took out my cigarettes and tried to light one. I got it done only because Swift held my head steady and Prager lit the match. Then I helped them through the same routine and we sat there, smoking away as though our lives depended on it.

"It's not a good idea," said Prager, finally.

"Why?"

"They'll arrest you. Don't laugh! You won't be dealing with a police force there. That's Washington. They'll get the army after you."

"Please shut up," I begged Prager.

Too late, I saw.

"Will they follow me underground?" the Professor grinned. "You're all wrong. What's government? Money! Who controls the gold supply controls the currency value. Controls economic stability! If I get all the money, I won't return it until they do what I say! Production for use! No gold lying around! No idle—"

"But it weighs thousands of tons!" Swift interjected.

"No hurry. They can't stop me. They can't hide it. I'll eat it out from underneath. Won't even notice it until I've got most of it. Don't think they count it every day, do you?"

"But it's kept in chambers…" I started to say and stopped. I'd been about to say it was kept in chambers of the toughest steel imbedded in huge layers of concrete. I finished, "…in chambers guarded by an elaborate alarm system, with underground rivers all around it…"

He was grinning. Just standing there and grinning.

BUT we kept after him, Varsag and I, trying to talk him out of it. I could see what Varsag's motive had been until now; he had simply stalled for time, inventing whatever slight pretext came to mind to keep him from leaving for Fort Knox. Tonight he had a new one—he was trying to interest the Professor in knocking off the Manhattan Savings Bank! I tell you it was weird sitting there and listening to Dr. Varsag calmly, reasonably discussing the merits behind his idea of having that bank robbed, hearing him comment on such matters as burglar alarms and capital known to be on hand, and the value of more practice before he undertook something as great as the Fort Knox repositories.

The Professor interrupted only once, lost in his own thoughts. He glanced at Swift and said, "Tons and tons of money, eh? Mountains of it?" Then he added, roguishly, "That's making mountains out of a mole, isn't it?" That, and his proud grin, was all he offered in rebuttal.

After awhile he yawned, got up, and painfully stretched his back, making odd little sounds. Without another word, he picked up his bags of tools, leaving the money behind, and walked out of the room.

"He's gone to sleep," said Varsag. "In my cellar, probably."

"As long as he stays there."

"Yes, Buzz, but how long will he stay there? You know the way he behaves. He doesn't say anything; he denies nothing—he just does what he pleases, whenever he pleases."

"We might try trussing him up, even chaining him, unless…"

"Unless what?" said Varsag. "Unless I was afraid of the effect it might have on him? It might very well wreck his orientation beyond possible repair. I'm well aware of that. Yet, in view of his latest aberration, I would take the chance if I believed there was any hope of tying or chaining him. You don't believe me?"

"'Let's say I don't agree with you, Doctor," I said. "There must be some way of—"

"Listen to me," said Varsag, soberly.

"You're not dealing with the Professor any more. In him you have a new being, with the strength of twenty men, with the agility of a cat, with the cunning and instincts of a highly intelligent animal. Force alone would have to be of such an overwhelming nature as to pin him for the long minutes necessary to apply your complete bonds, which I doubt possible. And to—"

"We might sneak up on him, catch him unawares," I interrupted. "The element of surprise…"

"I was coming to that. There is no such thing as finding him unawares. He lives in a state of perpetual alarm. His hearing is so fantastically acute that no sight could hope to match it. But suppose you could catch him—then what? He could snap ordinary bonds, even of stout rope, with scarcely much effort. And chains have to be anchored somewhere. Don't think of him as being completely dependent on his tools. His hands alone, added to his mole's understanding and intelligence, could probably undermine or uproot whatever anchors we devised."

The Doctor nodded grimly. "So you see the extent of your problem. I've thought about it before, and the meager chance of success it offers weighed against the possible harm that an unsuccessful attempt might do—well, I decided the best, and in fact, the only, chance of restraining him lay in trying to reason with him, to offer him new goals, to postpone his plan. But that's what I wanted to see you about. It was my hope that you would help me, if you could…if you will. I don't know if I am acting wisely."

"Do you want my opinion, Doctor?"

"By all means."

"I am not debating the wisdom of your choice, but if the choice were mine, I'd use force. I'm not sure how just yet. Maybe we could stun him, hit him over the head—we might even try chloroform if we got him down. Or you might try inducing him to undergo another supposed operation and anaesthetize him. Then we'd chain his wrists and feet and waist—fifteen separate chains if necessary—and then we'd all take turns on constant guard duty, twenty-four hours a day. How does that sound? Is there anything to talk over in that idea?"

Well, it sounded fine, and we did talk it over. We planned the operation scheme and two alternatives, only we never got a chance to try any of them. Because that night was the last time we saw the Professor until it was all over.

The next day—that was the day the papers ran the story of the Midtown Citizen's Bank having been robbed of $80,000 the night before—the three of us temporarily moved into Dr.

Varsag's house, ready for the first opportunity. We told Steiner the bare outlines of the Professor's project, and, probably due to his weakened, hysterical condition, he passed out cold. Later that day I went to the bank and withdrew an even twenty-five thousand dollars and gave it to him. Then I got a private ambulance to drive him to LaGuardia Airport and bought him a ticket to Quebec. The last I saw of him was a minute before the plane was ready to take off, its last announcement made. The ambulance doors opened and he streaked under the promenade and into the plane.

I had returned the compliment.

I didn't dream that in a little while I would be following him.

THE work the Professor did to get into the gold chambers of Fort Knox is a matter of record now, yet I wonder whether anyone who never knew the Professor can really understand what happened to him during that epochal achievement. I based part of this recital on my own familiarity with him, and partly upon what he later told Varsag, who, in turn, told me. Those were the darkest days, of course—but I will come to that presently.

The Professor left for Kentucky that next night. He took a private room on a sleeper. Ten miles from the gold chambers of Fort Knox he entered the earth. Fired by the magnitude of the task before him, he worked steadily for three days, with no sleep, with no food, with nothing but rare pools of water to refuel the prodigious energies that went into his furious labor. The galleries, drainages, miles of main and subsidiary tunneling, the ventilation and dirt disposal, are considered one of the truly great engineering miracles of our time.

I can see him when, at last, he was ready to bore through the main protective walls. His keen ears heard every footfall above the roofing of his tunnel, no sentry's turn unknown, no rolling wheel a mystery. He fumbled in one of his bags and brought out a small torch, to which steel was like wax. A flick of the wheel, sparks from the flint, and the torch was ready! In the steady, yellow-blue flare of light his face was an eerie mask of fatigue, a little, half-blind man in a suit of moleskin, hunched over, following the path his torch cut for him.

His muscles rebelled as the hours went by, but he forced their obedience. His face was inflamed from the searing heat of the torch. After the first steel walls, there was concrete again, and the pulverizing, swirling white clouds of dust that flew from his drill stabbed his tortured skin like thousands of daggers. Steel again, and concrete again, and steel again. And weariness sweeping over him in waves, his tools falling from limp hands, his eyeballs like live coals, his face a mass of torn blisters.

And then the flame whistling hollowly as he holed through! He crawled through and lay down, then crept about the vault until he felt the great steel doors. He tapped his tools on the floor faintly, and the echoes described the vault to him, its shape and dimensions. He found huge lockers filled with currency, incalculable fortunes in gold certificates, but worthless to him in his quest for bullion. Hour after hour he bored through the vaults, finding nothing but currency or small piles of bullion.

He had nothing to guide him, for there was no instinct to lead him to gold, and his only recourse was to keep going on and on, through chamber after chamber. No one knows how many hours he spent in his huge concentric circling of the inner vaults, but when he had been underground for almost seventy hours, he was completely drained of energy.

The chamber was comfortably warm.

Hand over hand he dragged himself to a corner. He broke open his last steel locker, and currency poured over him. His brain was lost in clouds of fatigue; his body was numb. Some last warning instinct whispered to him to go back, and he tried...

Guards found him the next day, curled up on loose bunches of gold certificates, as if they were a nest.

CHAPTER EIGHT

THE rest of this story isn't mine. It belongs to Dr. Varsag and to the Professor. I wasn't there when it happened, and I didn't know it was over until long afterward; weeks, I guess. But since I've told you this much, I want to tell you the rest. Especially because of the Professor.

The papers, you know, didn't learn about the Professor having been found in the Fort Knox vaults until several days later. We knew before they did. The F.B.I. and the Treasury Department's Secret Service came in and batted their poor heads against the problem, and the first break came when the Professor finally spoke, asking for Varsag. So, quietly, the F.B.I. and the S.S. called on the Doctor.

We were still living in his house, waiting for the Professor in forlorn hope, when they came. It was dinnertime, and that alone saved us. For Varsag, excusing himself, came back into the dining room told us instantly that the appalling worst had happened, and led us to the door and escape with apologies that the agents could hear, as if we had been casual dinner guests from whom he now was forced to excuse himself.

I don't know what he told them, but he stalled them long enough for me to withdraw the rest of my bank balance the next morning, and by afternoon, Swift, Prager, and I were on our way to Montreal. It was the first and quickest way out of the country.

Perhaps we shouldn't have gone. I felt that we were deserting Dr. Varsag, but there had been no time to argue and he had disposed of us swiftly, while we were still bewildered. We talked it over that night, waiting for the bank to open, and in the end I suppose it was Prager's wailing as much as anything else that decided us. We were afraid to allow him to remain in the country, and afraid to let him go alone. And, sentiment aside, at least for me, Dr. Varsag was right. He said there was nothing we could do for him, and that we risked being involved in a matter that we could only complicate.

And he was right again. Two days later the story broke in the papers. Nothing about Dr. Varsag or Steiner, or any of us—indeed, from the beginning to the end, until it was long over, our relation to these events, including Steiner and Varsag, remained a carefully guarded secret of the government. For when the story of the Professor having been found in the vault broke, Steiner's old gang blew everything they knew to the F.B.I. They were immediately sealed in the can as material witnesses under bail totaling half a million, and the hunt was on for Steiner and the three of us.

Very quietly. Without any warrants being issued. Without a single Wanted poster printed. But they were after us and we knew it. They were out to build up a case against Dr. Varsag and they realized what they were up against. Steiner's old gang weren't the kind of witnesses they could do anything with—they didn't know anything except that Steiner and probably we three knew everything. We hoped Steiner was safe, and we made sure we were. We bought second hand fishing clothes and a rattletrap and went deep into French Canada, to a little hamlet on the coast.

We stayed there until they found us, and we were half-glad they did. At times we had thought we would spend the rest of our lives there. Prager married a cute, fat little girl and went out herring fishing with her old man, and adopted the elegant name of Stanley. When Swift and I weren't visiting him, we were discussing plans for getting away to South America. And we might have gone if they hadn't found us.

But I'll tell you about the Professor and Dr. Varsag…

THEY didn't do anything to him at all. They had their plans and they waited while they searched for us. They issued no statements and contradicted no theories. There were items in Broadway gossip columns and Washington dope columns that the entire Fort Knox story was a fake. There were other stories that it was all true, and the Steiner gang was being held as accomplices as well as material witnesses— though they never were called the Steiner gang; his name was never mentioned. The F.B.I. went about its business, saying absolutely nothing, waiting.

Of course they tailed Dr. Varsag and they tapped his phone. He had gone with them to the Federal jail in New York where they brought the Professor, and after that first time, he visited him frequently. The F.B.I. put no obstacles in his way. Varsag knew they had the cell all nicely wired for sound, but they never heard anything he wanted to keep secret. Interesting, the way he did it. He merely breathed his important questions, and the Professor's wonderful hearing did the rest. He could generally answer by either nodding or shaking his head.

You see, the Doctor was waiting too. He had not admitted anything, and the Professor had not said anything. Yes, he had known a man named Steiner, had lived with him upstate in Woodbourne, along with some others. He had met them through mutual friends who seemed to be out of town. The Professor liked him—that was why he sent for him.

You know what he was waiting for? For the complete change in the Professor to become apparent. Given up hope? The farthest thing from it. He was more sure than ever that he was right! Only there was a bitter irony in his being right then, in the way it had happened. It must have been hard for him.

Because he could have gotten the Professor out of that jail in a hurry, by just saying so, by just helping him the least bit, if the Professor needed help.

There was no jail on earth that could hold the Professor. When they had caught him at first, he had been so weakened that he couldn't resist. The first few days they fed him so little, according to his needs, that he became ill. He had been eating twice what a normal man could eat, yet the doctor who examined him was forced to diagnose his condition as due to malnutrition bordering on starvation. His jailers, special agents from the F.B.I., fed him all he could eat after that. Some days there would be groups of doctors and F.B.I. officials watching the Professor eat. They still didn't know what they had caught. They had his tools, some of them, and part of the story, and they were trying to understand something that was still a little beyond them.

BUT they listened to Varsag's suggestions and fed him properly, and kept his cell dim, and provided him with bits of wood and cheap, ten-cent store saws and hammers and things, and from these the Professor built magnificent trestles and castles and elaborate puzzles. His brain and his hands needed something to tap the huge energy and power that had returned to him with the resumption of his proper diet. The F.B.I. never dreamt that they had rehabilitated the monster in their midst.

So what kept him there? What kept this being, locked in a cell that was a handful of matchsticks to him if he had wanted to escape? *If he had wanted to escape.* He didn't. That was it, you see. Varsag later explained it to me.

"I saw him those first days when his strength was returning to him, when the cunning, as I thought, was reviving in his brain. But the imprisonment had done something to him he didn't fathom. He had known that he had been doing things that were in conflict with the law. He had laughed at the police and Federal authority. But always, in the back of his mind, was the rationalization that he was helping society, that he was a benevolent member of it.

"But here, in his first helpless days, he had come into direct contact with the forces of the law, and in his every treatment, in every remark addressed to him, in every glance, he saw himself treated as an enemy of society. It awoke dim remembrances of another being in him, a being who had always been opposed to society, and against whose existence every fiber in him rebelled. He could not reconcile the two at first. If he tried to rationalize, telling himself he was misunderstood, he could not make the rationalization strong enough to overcome the deep repugnance that his imprisonment brought.

"I didn't make it easier for him. At first I let him sense from my manner that I considered him among the enemies of society. Then I let him realize how he had jeopardized not only me, but all his plans. When he felt his strength coming back and suggested—the barest fragment of a suggestion—escaping, I left him and didn't come back for two days. He did a lot of thinking in those two days, and by the time I saw him again, I knew the long awaited crisis was past.

"It was after that that I asked for him to be given materials to keep him busy. By the time he had saw and hammers and nails, dangerous weapons in his hands if they had guessed it, he had left the thought of escape behind. From then on I spoke to him a little each day, always truthfully, telling him that I had never agreed with him, that I had gone along with him waiting for his recovery. He could understand me then, and the truth was a powerful medicine, but it was what he needed.

"Only after I was completely sure of him did I begin to undertake the final step—a step which I knew was so finely shaded in the adjustment he would have to make, that I might undo everything. I began to prepare him for his ultimate escape.

"It was absolutely necessary. I didn't know when I would ask it of him, and I prayed that you would not be caught until the chance had come, but I knew it had to be. For in his present state, the Professor was a complete vindication of himself and everything he had done. Only by some action could he prove himself and my theories. What it was, I didn't know, beyond certain ideas I had. But I tried to make him see it, and little by little I succeeded. His faith and trust in me sometimes brought tears to my eyes. But he was happy those days. The animal fog that had enveloped his brain was gone. In all respects he was the old Professor again—not the thief, but the essential man, the new man, if you will, but a man not an animal.

"That had always been at the basis of my brother's and my own theories—that the man would remain a man, with these new resources added to his own, to be called upon when needed. And now, with final success in sight, with no permanent damage done, I waited for our chance with growing impatience.

"When the chance came it was as if the hand of Providence had reached down and tapped me on the shoulder. For in the midst of death and destruction, the way was clear for us to perform a miracle. The hand of Providence, I say, because such a cause had been one of the very thoughts I had had in consenting to create such a thing as a mole-man..."

ON AUGUST 8th, the so-called Black Hell mine, largest of the several Rockford mines in Pennsylvania, blew up. The number 14 tunnel was blasting that morning. One of the charges shook loose a section of the tunnel walls, which hit a dynamite wagon and smashed the rest of the tunnel to bits. The second explosion thundered along the main C shaft, wreaking havoc. Supports all along the 8th, 9th, 11th, 13th, and 14th tunnels crumbled, and thousands of tons of coal and timber crashed down on every available exit. Reinforced drainage canals on the 10th and 12th tunnel levels shattered, and the vast underground torrents roared down on the blocked exits and began eating through. More than eleven hundred miners were entombed hundreds of feet underground, faced with slow suffocation if the water did not break through and drown them all first.

By mid-afternoon, just about the time when Varsag was showing the newspaper headlines to the Professor, the Rockford engineers had completed their second survey and declared the situation almost hopeless. For the men in the 8th and 9th tunnels there was a slim chance, for the others none. Their opinion, of course confidential at the time, was of vast importance later on.

Varsag's first inclination was to go to the authorities and beg for the Professor's release; even then he wanted to avoid having the Professor break out. But he faced the situation realistically. Even if such consent could be won, it might not be before priceless time had been wasted. And he had little faith that he could win consent. Hardly anyone understood the Professor's capabilities, and they might never allow the Professor to touch his strange tools. He went directly to the prison himself.

After weeks of visiting the Professor, he was no longer so carefully searched. From the tools that the Professor had left behind—Varsag had hidden them, together with the stolen money, in one of the Professor's concealed tunnels in the cellar—he brought several to the cell, hidden about his person. A torch lay strapped against one leg by double garters, drills and bits in his other trouser leg. His vest pockets were filled with small pieces of machinery, and all these were added to the already formidable collection of seemingly harmless tools that the Professor had. Dr. Varsag was taking no chances.

The Professor understood the minute he saw the newspaper. In the shaded, gloomy cell, it was the work of a moment to secrete his new tools among the models he had built, and after the Doctor left, he waited only for his early evening meal before he assembled his tools.

Shortly before seven that night, he darted into the Varsag cellar, picked up the rest of his tools, the large powerful ones he would need, and was gone. At that very moment the house upstairs was filled with F.B.I. men who were questioning Varsag and beginning to search the house. At midnight, judging his time carefully, Dr. Varsag told them he wanted to go to Rockford, Pennsylvania. It was his opinion that the Professor might be found there. Only the sound judgment of Inspector Ivern, who quietly consented to the strange request, enabled the Doctor to be on the scene by dawn. Even then, most of it was already over. He came in time to witness the end.

What the Professor did that night and the next day has already been told by many of the survivors of that disaster.

He first appeared in the number 11 tunnel. Starting in an open field half a mile from the Black Hell mine, he had burrowed down on a forty-five degree angle until he could sense the water. He dug all around it, sometimes in circles, sometimes in long, convoluted double S shapes, burrowing through soft earth, drilling through rock and slate and coal, burning through timber, and when he first heard voices he had gone past the upper levels and reached the eleventh.

There was already two feet of water along the bottom of the tunnel. On all sides men stood, leaning against the walls, the sound holding up the injured, some sitting high against the overhead on planks and braces. Again and again their quiet voices would join in a hymn, and against it would be the rhythmic, sharp tapping of a crowbar against the wall. They were taking turns in sending up the signal that they were alive down there, praying that they would be heard.

And then they heard something drilling, something that made the walls tremble a little, and every sound stopped, every breath was held. They heard it come and leave again, and then it returned, growing stronger, and suddenly bits began falling from one of the walls.

HOARSE shouts rang out as panic swept through the men. They had looked for rescue along the main shaft. Now they thought their own tunnel was beginning to cave in under the pressure of the water from the drainage canals on the 10th level. The noise—in their fear and exhaustion it might have been swirling water—stopped, and the wall held. But the moment they were calm and quiet again, the noises resumed, only to stop a second time as new shouts rang out.

Then it began again, and the wall began chipping away, and long slivers of coal fell into the water and black dust filled the air. But there was a design to it! The pieces were falling in a pattern! The fear-strained, exhausted men stood silently, their sweat-stained, grimy faces lit by the one feeble lamp they allowed, watching the hole open.

The instant it opened, a head popped into the tunnel. It was the face of a man, blackened and bruised, and it came through what all of them knew were great, unbroken depths of solid rock and coal and all the time that this little man took

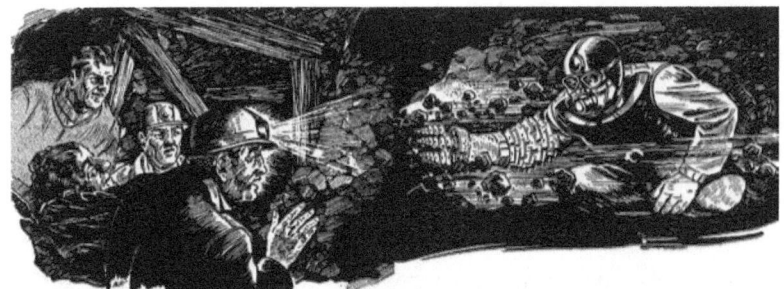

to enlarge the hole sufficiently for entry into the tunnel, they were as silent as the dead. They saw the dull-gleaming things he held in his hands and they saw that the little man's eyes were closed, and they watched him drop into the tunnel. He wore a suit that had once been white linen, and he had no shoes, and on his shoulders hung heavy, furry bags.

He stood among them and opened his eyes. "Follow the tunnel," he said. "It leads to the surface a half mile from here. I made it large enough for any of you. Go one at a time, but let someone stay here long enough to tell me how these tunnels lay."

Then he reached out and took the hand of a young boy who was being held by a grizzled old man, and he lifted him as if he was weightless and pushed him into the tunnel. "Go first," he said. "Don't be afraid. There isn't much time."

And since there had been no sound before, there was none now. It must have been strange to see the way those men received the gift of life from him, but it was understandable. With the directions he received, the Professor went down to the 13th level, and then up again through the 8th and 9th, connecting them all to his own slanted tunnel. And though underground all was still while hundreds of men, tired and wounded and afraid, crawled through the earth to emerge under the sky once more, it was different above ground when the first survivors came up, to run back to Rockford and the mineshaft and tell their incredible story.

When the first fierce shouts of rejoicing were over, and the story itself was told, thousands went to the field where the little tunnel lay like an innocent hole in the ground. By the light of torches and great fires, the survivors were fed and dressed and the injured were treated, for none would leave the spot. Again and again frenzied shouts rang out from thousands of voices as a new group would come out of the dark tombs, and always there were anxious questions about the little man who was still down there, still burrowing. And the story they told was always the same...

By the time Dr. Varsag arrived on the scene, more than a thousand men had been brought up. The story had gone out by radio all over the country, and from everywhere people came pouring into that mining town in Pennsylvania. They flew in from Chicago newspapers in planes; they clogged the roads for miles in cars. By morning the State Troopers had called out the National Guard to keep order. There were more than forty thousand people there, waiting in the fields.

You remember the picture of the Professor coming out of the ground. The sun was just coming over a flaming horizon, its light reflected against the Troopers' boots that were at the top of the picture. He was halfway out, his hands stretched out to lift himself up, and a circle of fifty reaching hands going toward him. His eyes were closed, but that was because of the flash bulbs. There was utter weariness on his face, but it was hard to see except in the closest pictures because it was so blackened.

They held back the wild crowds and wrapped him in blankets, and Varsag was there beside him. But all the Professor wanted was food.

"I must go back," he whispered. "There are still others in the number 14 tunnel. There's water all around them, but I'll dig under and I'll bring them up. All I want now is food."

And while he ate he studied the charts of the mine they brought him, his eyes burning from the brilliant sunlight, his ears crashing with the sounds of so many people. When he had finished eating, he lay down on the ground for five minutes and closed his eyes. Then he picked up his bags of tools, and without speaking to anyone, he went into the ground again while Varsag stood there mute, the tears streaming down his face. He wasn't the only one in tears.

WELL, you know the rest. When the Professor had done all he could, he had saved the lives of all but forty of those who had survived the explosions. Including those, the death toll among the miners was seventy, and the Professor made it seventy-one. He gave his life to bring out twelve of the men from the number 14 tunnel, and he must have known he was taking that chance when he went down again.

Sometime later, when the searching parties were able to penetrate into that part of the mine, they reconstructed the manner in which he had probably met his death. He had been dead almost a month by then, of course, so it was hard to know for certain. They found him lying near his tunnel into the flooded level, with a beam across his back. It was an ordinary beam from the roof, and it weighed no more than thirty pounds or so, but it had smashed down on him and broken his back. They said there was a good chance that it hadn't killed him, but that he had lain there paralyzed and helpless until the water came through and he drowned with the others. They were separated from him by a wall less than a foot's breadth, and in a minute more, had he been able to, he would have broken through to them.

Even a mole, you see, couldn't make predictions about a tunnel it hadn't built for itself...

I guess that's about all, except for the trial maybe, and a few details, if you're interested.

They had their trial, after all. Too much public clamor for it, so they had to go through with it, feeling like fools, I suppose, though they'd done nothing but their jobs. Because the public made that trial the occasion for one of the biggest public celebrations they ever had in Frankfort, Kentucky. Yes, they held it near the site of his exploit in the Fort Knox vaults, about which everybody knew by then. Pennsylvania fought to have it there, but Kentucky had the law on its side. I understand Pennsylvania flew all state flags at half-mast for a month from that day on. I wasn't there, if you remember.

I understand the feeling was so high that it almost got Steiner and his bunch a pardon. But I don't think he could complain much. They nailed him on a dozen technical counts, but he'll be out in a few years. Varsag says when the time comes he'll do what he can with the parole board, but I think this is one time he'll listen to me.

Why, his time alone these days is too valuable to waste on Steiner, except maybe in rat experiments. That laboratory they built Dr. Varsag—you know, the Arnold Varsag Memorial Research Institute, to which all those banks and others contributed—keeps him so busy his head is spinning. What's he doing there? You don't really expect me to tell you, do you? I didn't think so. Let's just say you'll hear from him one of these days. Between his volunteer Lightfinger Brigade (nice name, don't you think?) and the tools and things he's got to work out...well, he's busy, let's say.

And so am I. Swifto and I are going up to Canada in a couple of days, to be witnesses for the defense. They never heard about the Professor up there. What defense? Prager's! His wife's father is suing him for having to support his daughter all the time Prager was kept in Kentucky, testifying at the trial. Comes to almost forty dollars, and that's a lot of herring, though Prager says he just doesn't like the principle of the thing.

With us on his side he can't win. But we'll pay the forty dollars for him if he'll let us experiment on him before he becomes a father. No, it's not him we're thinking about—it's the children, and that's a job for a genius like Varsag.

Any more questions?

THE END

If you've enjoyed this book, you will not want to miss these terrific titles...

ARMCHAIR SCI-FI & HORROR DOUBLE NOVELS, $12.95 each

D-141 **ALL HEROES ARE HATED** by Milton Lesser
AND THE STARS REMAIN by Bryan Berry

D-142 **LAST CALL FOR DOOMSDAY** by Edmond Hamilton
THE HUNTRESS OF AKKAN by Robert Moore Williams

D-143 **THE MOON PIRATES** by Neil R. Jones
CALLISTO AT WAR by Harl Vincent

D-144 **THUNDER IN THE DAWN** by Henry Kuttner
THE UNCANNY EXPERIMENTS OF DR. VARSAG by David V. Reed

D-145 **A PATTERN FOR MONSTERS** by Randall Garrett
STAR SURGEON by Alan E Nourse

D-146 **THE ATOM CURTAIN** by Nick Boddie Williams
WARLOCK OF SHARRADOR by Gardner F. Fox

D-148 **SECRET OF THE LOST PLANET** by David Wright O'Brien
TELEVISION HILL by George McLociard

D-147 **INTO THE GREEN PRISM** by A Hyatt Verrill
WANDERERS OF THE WOLF-MOON by Nelson S. Bond

D-149 **MINIONS OF THE TIGER** by Chester S. Geier
FOUNDING FATHER by J. F. Bone

D-150 **THE INVISIBLE MAN** by H. G. Wells
THE ISLAND OF DR. MOREAU by H. G. Wells

ARMCHAIR SCIENCE FICTION CLASSICS, $12.95 each

C-61 **THE SHAVER MYSTERY, Book Six**
by Richard. S. Shaver

C-62 **CADUCEUS WILD**
by Ward Moore & Robert Bradford

ARMCHAIR MYSTERY-CRIME DOUBLE NOVELS, $12.95 each

B-1 **THE DEADLY PICK-UP** by Milton Ozaki
KILLER TAKE ALL by James O. Causey

B-2 **THE VIOLENT ONES** by E. Howard Hunt
HIGH HEEL HOMICIDE by Frederick C. Davis

B-3 **FURY ON SUNDAY** by Richard Matheson
THE AGONY COLUMN by Earl Derr Biggers

www.ingramcontent.com/pod-product-compliance
Lightning Source LLC
Chambersburg PA
CBHW050043180626
46810CB00002B/873